NASTY LEFTOVERS

By

Guy L. Pace

Copyright © 2016 Guy L. Pace

Cover Design by Scott Deyett

Edited by Brandi Midkiff

Zondervan is granting permission for the latest edition of the NIV text only (currently 2011), available for personal use at http://www.zondervan.com, http://www.biblica.com, http://www.biblegateway.com and http://www.youversion.com. We are not granting permission for use of the earlier editions or version of the NIV text. For more information, please visit the following website: http://www.biblica.com/en-us/the-niv-bible/previous-editions/

This is a work of fiction. Names, characters, places, brands, media, and incidents are either the product of the author's imagination or are used fictitiously. Any resemblance to similarly named places or to persons living or deceased is unintentional.

ISBN :0-9978669-1-8
ISBN13: 978-0-9978669-1-9

Library of Congress Control Number: 2016934384

Acknowledgements

I want to acknowledge the efforts of friends and teammates who struggled through the early drafts of this sequel with me. Doc Kane, who got to read the really ugly first draft (you ought to see it now, Doc!). Heather Huffman: the Vox Dei imprint manager, whose faith in me sets the bar pretty high. My team at Vox Dei: Brandi Midkiff, editor; Sophie Thomas, proofreader; and Scott Deyett, cover designer. I couldn't ask for more professional, talented, and hard- working people. And here's to Becki Brannen, whose job it is to herd the book through the final production process and marketing. Thanks, all of you. It has been a great ride. Of course, all glory goes to God.

To Connie, once again. My first reader,

my inspiration, and my primary support system.

ONE

Changes

PAUL SHANNON CROSSED the finish line, recording his best ever time for the mile.

He slowed and continued to jog around the track, cooling down. As he came around the far side he saw the line of trees where last year the coyote—the Adversary—had appeared to him for the first time. The memory sent a chill down his spine.

Solar panels glared from the roofs of nearby houses, and propellers of wind generators quietly spun over the abundance of the household gardens that had replaced lawns in recent months. He saw rainwater barrels beneath eaves and downspouts, storing water for the gardens and livestock. Every house had chickens; some had a goat or two. Fresh food no longer came in by truck. What his family couldn't grow for themselves, they traded for in the community market. Many in the community specialized in certain crafts or other skills and traded their products and services for food and other daily supplies.

Conventional electrical power was a thing of the past. The town now limped along on power from a nearby nuclear plant, but even that was available only sporadically. The people who maintained the plant and the existing distribution lines could only do so much. They were paid in food and other goods. Across the nation, individual communities were cut off from each other, forced to sustain themselves. Overall, Paul's community was holding itself together with faith, determination, and grit.

Ten months earlier, the Adversary had unleashed chaos and destruction on the world, and Paul had been tasked with setting things right. His best friends, Amy Grossman and Joe Banes, joined him on his dangerous cross-country trek to reset reality. Through everything—zombies, killer monks, Samurai, aliens, and the Adversary himself—they stayed faithful to God's mission. But setting things right didn't mean setting things back to what they'd been. Joe was gone, killed by an alien blaster. More than two-thirds of the world's population had died or disappeared. Entire cities had vanished outright. Survivors struggled to rebuild their lives among the ruins of failed infrastructure and collapsed governments.

Paul headed to the showers. He missed Joe. They used to make this walk together at the end of the physical education period. Even now, after all these months, he still found himself turning and expecting to find his old friend faithfully at his side with a joke or pithy comment. That would never happen again. Some hurts just couldn't heal this side of Heaven.

But others could, and starting tomorrow, Paul was going to help with that.

#

Showered and dressed, Paul shouldered his backpack and headed to the hall to clear out his locker. This was the last day of term. After the Troubles, teachers and students had limped through the remainder of the school year as best they could, so there wasn't much left in his locker now, just a couple of notebooks, some pens and pencils, and a jacket. He stuffed it all in the pack and went to the main entrance.

Amy Grossman stood near the door talking with some friends. They chatted animatedly as he approached. A warm glow filled him as he watched her grey eyes flashing with her ready smile. She talked rapid-fire and brushed at her auburn hair when it fell across her face.

"Are you ready to go?" Paul said, interrupting. "We have a lot of packing to do for the mission trip."

Amy turned and smiled up at him. He felt himself blush. He was taller than Amy now, and he liked it.

"Yep!" she said. "Locker is empty and I'm ready to leave this place for the summer."

Paul said his goodbyes to Amy's friends and they left.

The route home had not changed since the Troubles. When they reached the small wooden bridge, Amy stopped.

"Remember that troll?" she said. "He was so snotty and droolly and warty and disgusting. And he wouldn't stop talking about making us into stew. Every time I see this bridge, I keep expecting another troll to show up."

"He wasn't the only one who wanted to eat us," Paul said as he stepped onto the bridge. "That old witch with the gingerbread house was seriously disturbing. Too bad you slept through that. The enchanted candy knocked you right out."

"I was awake for the swamp monster, at least. We never got a good look at it, but it sure did enjoy munching on the goblins we knocked into the water."

They stopped on the other side of the little bridge, and Paul smiled at Amy. "We encountered some pretty nasty stuff, didn't we?"

"Yeah, but it wasn't all horrible. Mostly, but not all. Gabriel. I liked him."

"Me, too. I wonder what he's doing these days."

"Can't imagine. Angel stuff, I guess."

"Angel stuff?" Paul grinned and nudged her shoulder. "That must be a technical Angel term."

They walked in comfortable silence for a while. Then Amy said, "We haven't talked about what we're taking on this trip."

Paul shrugged. "What is there to talk about? Do you have an itemized list of your outfits?"

She gave him a withering look.

"No." She looked away and then back. "Well, yes, but that's not what I mean. You need to bring your sword. And we should bring both our staffs."

"What do you expect we'll find on this trip? Monsters?"

"I don't know. But we're going into a place that was devastated by the Adversary. I think we should be prepared."

Paul stopped walking. He'd acquired his sword late in last year's mission, in a real-life role-playing game complete with medieval village, brigands, and red-eyed wolves. The sword had helped him finish his task, and he knew he'd always treasure it, but he hadn't expected to ever use it again.

"What's wrong?" Amy asked.

"Nothing. It's just … well, this is an official church-sponsored mission trip. With families and itineraries and caravans. I don't know how people would feel about me bringing a large, dangerous edged weapon along. Besides, the monsters are gone. Aren't they? Wasn't that the whole point of last year's mission? This trip is about cleaning up some the mess the Adversary left behind."

"You don't think you should bring the sword?"

Paul sighed. He knew she was right.

"Actually … yeah, you're right. And that's what worries me. We don't know what we're going to run into when we reach the capital, or even before then. I really wasn't trying to argue with you. Really. I was just trying to convince myself."

"I think you know what I mean," Amy said.

"You do?" Paul wasn't certain he knew what he meant.

"Sure. Last year when we were so far from home and fighting one bizarre thing after another, I kept longing for things to get back to normal. But now we're home, and what is normal anymore?"

"Exactly. Which reminds me of another thing." He paused a moment. "This might sound crazy. I don't know why I feel this way, but sometimes I think back on that time when it was just you, me, and Joe, never knowing where our next meal or our next ride would come along—living in constant danger, and constantly praying for God's protection and guidance, and … I kind of miss it."

"So do I."

He smiled at her. Amy always understood.

"Well, I'd better go," she said. Their ways parted here. "Come over later?"

"You bet."

#

As Paul entered the house he was met by a small, noisy boy.

"We goin' on a trip, Paul!"

"I know, Roger Rabbit!" He grabbed the little boy and hugged him. "We will have so much fun!"

"We goin' to Washinden!"

"That's right! Washington, D.C., the once and future capital of the United States!"

"Mom said we're on a mission! Like secret agents!" Roger's face was alight with wonder and excitement.

"And all your friends from church will be going along, too!" Paul said.

He was glad to see his little brother so excited about the mission. He only hoped the excitement would last. This would be no trip to an amusement park. It was going to be a lot of work. Paul wasn't sure how the young kids were going to fit in with that.

He put Roger down and they went to the kitchen, where he found his mother was deep in a cleaning frenzy. She wiped sweat from her forehead with a paper towel.

"I just brought the last of the laundry in from the line. The rest of the family is all packed, and you have plenty of clean clothes in your room, so pack your suitcase and anything else you plan to bring. I suppose you'll be bringing your pad and games." She threw him a hard look and pushed a stray, black curl out of her face. "I have dinner in the oven. We'll eat in a couple hours and have an early bedtime. So get busy!"

"Yes, ma'am!" Paul said and saluted.

"Don't be cute!"

Upstairs in his room, Paul dumped the contents of his pack on the bed. He rifled through it and took a notebook full of paper, a pen, and some pencils. He set those next to the pack. The rest of the school material he piled at the foot of his bed. None of that would go along. He then grabbed his small suitcase from the closet and started packing his freshly laundered clothing.

His backpack was new, since the Troubles. The old one had fallen apart shortly after he and Amy had returned from the mission. Paul now made a few modifications to the new pack. Using a piece of material from the old pack, he hand-sewed a place for the sword's leather sheath inside the new pack. The sheath would fit tightly down inside, with the sword hilt near enough to the top that he could easily grab it with his right hand and draw it out.

He picked up the Old Timer pocketknife from his dresser and held it a while. A man named Sal had given it to him last year near the end of his mission. It had been a gift from Sal's grandfather years earlier. Paul would never forget Sal's kindness in giving it to him, or in cooking breakfast for him and Amy that last morning before they'd gone into the enchanted forest to complete the mission.

The Old Timer went into his jeans pocket, and his tablet went into the protective sleeve in the backpack. Power adapters, cables, and other items went in the main compartment, as well.

He checked the closet one more time. On a hanger, looking out of place among the T-shirts and button-downs, was the leather vest he'd gotten at the same time as the sword.

He slid it off the hanger. The leather felt familiar, comfortable, in his hands. He hadn't put it on since his return, but he hadn't wanted to get rid of it either. He and that vest had been through a lot together.

Since returning home, about ten months ago, Paul had grown several inches. The jeans and shirts he wore during the Troubles no longer fit and had been handed down to younger boys in the community. On impulse, he tried on the vest.

It fit perfectly.

Okay, I'll bring it along, he thought. He started to take it off but decided to leave it on for now. It felt comforting, somehow.

Summer was on the way, but Paul included a UNC Tar Heel sweatshirt and a windbreaker jacket, just in case. Some determined academics, he'd heard, were trying to restore the University of North Carolina, but most people were focused on survival. Paul's dream of attending the university seemed pretty far off.

He looked over his gear and scanned his room one more time. He couldn't think of anything else he needed.

Then he saw a picture of Joe and himself taken on the Outer Banks during a family vacation when they were about thirteen. He sat on the edge of his bed, looking at the picture, remembering. Amy had taken the picture. That was a great vacation.

Not long before Paul and his friends had faced off against the aliens in the battle that cost Joe his life, they had driven near a black fog that covered Rapid City, South Dakota. The fog had seemed to be chasing them. A wisp of it had come through the open car window and touched Joe's arm. That one touch had been enough to send Joe into spasms of pain. Much later, Joe had said he now knew what hell was like. He hadn't gotten a chance to fully recover before the battle with the aliens. Paul often wondered whether Joe would still be alive today if he hadn't been weakened by that fog.

Before coming to Rapid City, the black fog had first descended on Washington, D.C. It had covered the entire city for days. After the Troubles, the fog had lifted from the capital, leaving some tortured survivors behind. The federal government now operated out of a facility near Denver, Colorado.

Earlier in the year, some intrepid souls from Paul's community had scouted the route to the former capital and the surrounding urban areas. They'd found survivors at various locations, mostly around the familiar landmarks and monuments. The mission was to go to the city and try to find and save those survivors. The trip would last most of the summer, according to the plan.

He tucked the picture inside the backpack, next to his tablet where it would stay flat.

#

When Paul finished his chores around the house—watering the garden, feeding chickens, and checking for eggs—he sat with the family for dinner. Later, he walked over to Amy's to visit. While they were gone on the mission trip, neighbors who were staying behind would keep all the houses secure, the gardens watered, and the animals fed and cared for.

A year ago, Paul and Amy—and Joe—would just get online and chat and then get involved in an online game. Now, the Internet existed only in some places and was no longer a world-wide anything. He and Amy would sometimes play games using a local wireless network, but their interest in and time for the games dropped as their roles in supporting the families increased.

"Hey," Amy said when she answered the door.

"Hey. I'm ready," he said. He held his arms out so Amy could see the vest.

"That's the leather vest?"

"Yeah."

"I thought you would have grown out of it this year," she said, putting her hands on the vest at his shoulders. "You're so much taller, broader ..." She quickly took her hands back and looked aside a moment.

Paul looked down at the vest and shrugged his shoulders. "I guess it grew with me."

"Hmmm, it's almost like it was made for you."

"Yeah," he said. "I can't stay, just wanted to come by for a minute. We have a family meeting."

"We do, too." She reached out and gently grasped his hand. "I'm bringing the little crystal vials. They don't have anything in them, but it seemed right to include them in my pack."

Paul thought of the Old Timer in his pocket and the picture in his pack. "I seem to need to bring some of the things from last year, too." He swallowed hard. "I miss Joe."

"Yeah. Me too. I'm glad we still have each other."

Paul gave her hand a little squeeze.

They sat on the porch and talked in the cool evening, reminiscing about last year's adventure and speculating about what they would find in D.C. Finally, Amy got up.

"It's getting cold and we have meetings," she said.

"Yeah. I'll see you tomorrow."

"Tomorrow," she said as he turned and left.

TWO

Travel

THE FAMILY SUV was packed to the top with luggage and sleeping bags. Paul buckled little Roger into his child seat in the quiet of the early dawn. Roger nodded out almost immediately.

"He'll sleep most of the way," Dad said as he climbed into the driver's seat.

Sarah, Paul's younger sister, climbed in behind Dad and buckled in. She clutched her favorite doll and a pillow.

Mom got in the front passenger seat and Paul buckled his belt in the seat behind her.

"The house is all locked up," she said.

"Mrs. Morgan will check on the garden, chickens, and everything else while we're gone," Dad said. "She has a key. I think we're all set."

He pulled out of the driveway and out into the street. The Grossmans, just a couple of blocks away, were getting into their car as the Shannons pulled up. Amy's father waved and said he would follow them to the meeting point. The participants in the mission were to meet at a shopping center parking lot near the freeway. They would caravan from there.

The Grossmans pulled out and followed the Shannons.

Mom looked in the back seat, checking Sarah and Roger. Then she looked at Paul and smiled.

"I can't get over how that vest still fits you perfectly after all that growing you did this year," she said. "You must have grown a foot since the Troubles. It's like the vest was made for you."

Paul fingered the hilt of the sword just inside his backpack on the floor. *Some mysteries are just that,* he thought.

#

At the shopping center parking lot, about thirty vehicles, some with gear bundled in racks on top, were clustered in an outside area. The people gathered in a group to the side with the mission leaders. Everyone deferred to one person, Ray Franklin, a church elder and the mission leader. Franklin was tall, grey-haired, and imposing, but Paul knew him as a gentle, caring man who had taught his Sunday school classes the last few years.

Franklin's bass voice boomed out over the crowd. "Randy, there, will pass each driver a numbered card." He pointed to a younger man who waved the numbered cards in the air. "The number on your card is your place in the caravan. Keep it on your dash. We need to keep in sequence to help keep track of everyone. The last thing we want to do is lose one of our families when we're on a mission to save some helpless souls."

There was some laughter and he waited for it to die down.

"We'll be linking up to Interstate 85 near Henderson, and taking Interstate 95 from Petersburg on north. We plan a rest stop just after we cross into Virginia and we'll stop as often as we can until we reach the hotel in Arlington. Our scouts—" he pointed to two other men standing nearby and they raised their hands—"checked out the route and the hotel and we should have no trouble getting through. There's a detour through Richmond, but we'll be prepared for that."

A murmur swept through the crowd and Elder Franklin paused until it calmed.

"We distributed some two-way radios and extra batteries to several of the cars. Those cars are marked with orange placards on the front and back. If there are problems, follow them and get instructions.

"We lost two-thirds of the world population during the Troubles," he went on. "Some places are completely depopulated. Some are like our community, still working and getting on. Others are more desperate and broken. We are doing what we can, but a lot of the political, government, and utility infrastructure is gone and it may be years before those things are rebuilt.

"With that said, please understand that we will do what we need to do to protect our families and our mission. The adults among you are properly trained and armed. We are prepared to deal with rogues or bandits, should we encounter any. With God's help and blessing, we will have an uneventful passage to Arlington. Let's pray."

He bowed his head and the crowd followed his example.

"Father, we come to You thankful for our blessings and good fortune. We know it is through our faith and Your grace that we have such abundance in our community. We are grateful for Your providence and the opportunity we have to serve on Your behalf. On this beautiful spring morning we ask Your blessings on our mission team as we prepare to leave. We expect to face challenges and difficulties, Father, and we ask for strength and wisdom to help us through those times. We know You will be with us as we try to save those lost souls in our former capital and help reopen that once great city. We do this, Father, for Your glory and in Your name. As in all things, Father, Your will be done. We ask these things in the name of Your Son, Jesus Christ. Amen."

The crowd chorused, "Amen."

The drivers queued up to Randy to get their numbered cards and everyone else headed to their cars.

Amy joined Paul.

"It sounds like they're expecting some trouble," she said.

"It does. I wonder if that detour in Richmond will be a problem."

"My dad brought a pistol and bullets."

"Both Mom and Dad have them," Paul said. "Dad got one of the radios." Paul saw Dad and Amy's father walking together. "Looks like we'll be close in the caravan, too."

"That makes me feel better." She gave him an appraising look. "That vest looks pretty good."

Paul felt his cheeks flush. "Thanks."

Amy headed to her family car. "I'll see you at the first stop."

#

Paul watched the North Carolina landscape pass by for a bit, then got out his tablet and played a game. He kept the power adapter plugged in so the tablet would stay charged. Roger and Sarah slept. Dad drove and Mom kept the radio and watched the sides of the road.

The two-way radio occasionally chirped with status checks, but no warnings or problems were reported.

The caravan was just rolling down old US Highway 1 past Wake Forest when the two-way chirped and instructions for a gas stop were shared. All vehicles would top off at a gas station near Youngsville. This was one of the few still functional gas stations on this route.

"We've only been on the road about a half-hour," Dad said.

"I heard the scouts say some of the gas stations along the Interstate were guarded by gangs," Mom said.

"Shh." Dad glanced in the mirror and saw Paul looking at him. Then he said to Paul, "Don't repeat that."

"Don't worry," Paul said. "I won't."

"Well," Mom said, "this will be a good bathroom stop, anyway."

As they pulled into the gas station, Paul tucked away the tablet. Randy was already out and directing cars, based on number, to the gas pumps. Adults dug out cash and paid attendants after topping off, then pulled into parking spots. The credit card slots on the pumps were taped over. Since the Troubles, credit card companies and their systems had ceased to function and no one accepted or used them anymore. Only cash was accepted, and gas was about the only thing cash was used for. Everything else—food, clothing—was on a barter system.

Paul headed to the men's room, then hung outside until he saw Amy. It was full daylight, but he felt a nervous tension in his back as he scanned the trees lining the rest area. It had been at a rest stop last year, late at night, when the Adversary had appeared to him in the guise of a coyote and spoken into his mind. He shivered from a chill at the thought. Reality had been reset, but the damage was done. Now he was involved in trying to restore their world.

He took a deep breath, then look up and saw Amy.

"My folks said the Virginia gas stations were run by gangs," Amy said as she walked up. "Good thing we're topping off here."

"I heard," Paul said, "and was told not to talk about it." He grinned and nudged her arm. "Like I could not share anything with you."

"Yeah."

"The sooner we get to Arlington, the sooner I'll feel better about the trip. There seems to be a lot of stuff the adults aren't telling us. But I don't think they would intentionally bring whole families into danger." He looked around at people getting back into their cars. "Would they?"

"I don't think so," Amy said and touched his arm. "I'll keep my ears open, in any case."

#

The caravan continued along Highway 1 to Henderson and joined Interstate 85 without stopping. Taking the Interstate didn't help the caravan speed. It was kept to about forty-five or fifty miles per hour due to abandoned vehicles and uncleared wrecks on the road.

Paul watched farmland and small towns go by. He dozed off at one point but was awakened by the two-way. They had crossed into Virginia and would stop at a rest stop just up the road.

Randy, again, was out directing cars into parking spots and keeping the caravan in order. People got out, stretched, used the facilities, ate snacks at the picnic tables, and generally enjoyed the spring day. No other cars or trucks were at the stop and they had seen no other traffic on the highway.

Paul and Amy joined some others their age around a table with some refreshments laid out.

"Yeah, they'd rather use these rest stops than go into a town," one of the boys said. "My dad says these are too far from towns and all, the gangs don't bother with 'em. Nothin' here to protect or hijack."

"I hear that the detour in Richmond may get dangerous," another boy said. "Gangs blocked a couple of the overpasses and we'll have to go through downtown Richmond to get around it."

"That's probably why all the adults brought guns," Paul offered. "This many people, armed. The bandits will probably leave us alone."

"I hope so," Amy said.

THREE

Ambush

ALMOST TWO HOURS later, the caravan pulled into another rest area just past Dinwiddie, Virginia. They followed the now-standard routine, with Randy directing the cars. After about fifteen minutes, Elder Franklin called everyone together in the grassy area of the rest stop.

"Friends," he said, raising his arms to quiet everyone down, "this next leg of the trip may be the most dangerous. When we get to Richmond, there will be a roadblock on the overpass just north of the James River. There is another block where Highway 1 crosses the Interstate. Our plan is to navigate to Broad Street, and take that west to Belvidere Street, then north, back to the Interstate.

"This is what we want you to do. When we cross the river, all windows will be down. All children will lie down in back seats or on the floor in back. All adults with guns will have them at ready, and pointing out windows, where appropriate. As we planned, this is just a show of force and we will not be shooting anyone…if it can be avoided. We will continue in caravan in this manner until we are back on the freeway and moving along. Are there any questions?"

One of the boys about Paul's age raised his hand. The elder nodded to him.

"Why are we rolling down the windows?" he asked.

"Two reasons," the Elder Franklin said. "First, for safety. If we get shot at, breaking glass can hurt the kids and other passengers. Second, so we can display how well armed we are."

He looked around the group for any other questions. No one raised a hand.

"We should have no problem getting through Petersburg and to the James River. I ask that everyone be prepared by the time we get to the river. Let's pray."

He bowed his head and the crowd followed suit.

"Father, this next leg will be a trial. We know You are with us and we pray for Your love and protection, the wisdom to act and respond with discretion and resolve, and the strength to see this through. We ask these things in the name of Your Son, Jesus Christ. Amen."

"Amen," came in a chorus from the group.

The caravan left the rest stop and continued down the highway. At Petersburg, they switched to Interstate 95 and continued north. The going was a little slower, as there were more disabled and abandoned vehicles. In a couple of places the caravan had to weave around and over the medians to get past obstructions. After almost an hour, Paul saw the James River on the east side of the freeway. Half an hour later, the caravan reached the bridge.

The two-way radio crackled and windows started going down. Paul got Roger and Sarah down on the floor in the back, then squeezed down next to them. It was tight and Roger wiggled around a lot.

"You know, I saw a lot of strange stuff when I went on my mission last year," Paul said, gently moving Roger's foot from his ribs. "But I don't remember anything as weird as the sight of my mom holding a Smith & Wesson .45 caliber pistol out the window of our Highlander."

Dad looked over at Mom and smiled. "Yeah, well, your mom's full of surprises. Are you and your brother and sister squared away back there?"

"Yep, we're all secure in our bunker here."

From his place in back, Paul could only see the sky through the windows. He felt the car leave the freeway and go down the ramp. Then they were on the city surface streets. Passage was slow and bumpy.

"I see some people up ahead," Mom said. She held her pistol in the window, braced against the door post. "They don't look armed, just standing around."

"I hope that's the worst we see," Dad said.

"I wanna see," Sarah cried out.

"You stay down," Dad said.

"Now we're on Broad," Mom said.

The caravan speed picked up a bit, and the car hit some harder bumps. Roger complained and wiggled around.

"Keep still, Roger Rabbit," Paul said and hugged his little brother. Sarah was curled up with her doll and pillow.

A popping sound came from up ahead.

"I hear popcorn," said Roger.

"It's gunfire," Dad said. "Paul! Keep them down!"

The two-way crackled.

"They tried to stop us at a choke point," a voice on the radio said. "We fired back and they ran. Keep an eye out. Don't slow down."

Paul heard his mom gasp, and then she fired three times. Sarah screamed and Roger wailed.

"Roger, Sarah, it's okay," Paul said. His hears rang from the sound of gunfire in the car. "Mom and Dad know what they're doing"

Mom got on the two-way and reported her encounter. Her voice shook a little. "Someone came out of an alley to our north and aimed a rifle at us. I scared him off. I may have winged him."

"I want to go home," Roger whimpered.

Paul did this best to reassure his little brother. Sarah helped, though Paul could see that she was almost as scared as Roger.

Some other gunfire erupted along the caravan, but just a few short bursts. Something clanged against the roof of their car; Paul guessed it was a wild bullet. The car bumped around some more and turned.

"That's Belvidere," Mom said. "We'll be back to the freeway soon."

After a few minutes, Paul, Roger, and Sarah were pressed against the left side of the car as they rounded up the on ramp. Paul made a big show of flattening himself agains the car door while saying, "Whoooaaaa!" Sarah laughed, and Roger giggled through his tears.

"Okay, you can get up," Dad said. "We're back on the freeway."

Paul helped Roger back into his car seat while Sara buckled her own seatbelt. "You guys did great," Paul told them. "You stayed down just like you were told and that helped a lot."

Mom and Dad added their praise, and then Paul and his parents let out a sigh of relief at the same moment.

The caravan picked up speed. The two-way relayed reports of a couple of minor wounds and a vehicle with engine problems.

"We have a huge open parking lot just ahead," a voice said on the radio, "at the Kings Dominion park. We'll pull in there and assess the damage. Keep weapons handy."

In a few minutes, the caravan wound into the huge parking lot, Randy directing the cars into a wide circle around a vehicle with steam and smoke coming from under the hood.

"Adults keep a watch on the perimeter. Bring the wounded to the elder's car for aid," Randy called out as cars moved past him.

The teens and younger kids moved toward the center of the circle, keeping out of the way as best they could. Paul noticed three large bullet holes in the front side of the smoking and steaming car. Two people—Dorothy James, the lady who played piano in church, and George Humphries, the older man who was always tending the church grounds—were being assisted to the back of the Elder Franklin's Suburban, where medical cases were open on the tailgate. George limped, with blood on his left leg. Dorothy held a rag against her right shoulder.

Other cars in the outer circle had bullet holes or gouges, but none seemed to be serious.

One of the teens in their group, Tom Smalls, gathered the younger children and started them singing "Zacchaeus Was a Wee Little Man." Paul thought it was interesting to see, since Tom was usually a quiet, reserved type and here he was leading a funny song and capering around in front of the little kids. He smiled, turned, and saw Steve Jefferson sitting on a park bench cuddling two toddlers in his lap. Steve was one of football linemen from their team, when there was a team. His large arms wrapped gently, protectively around the small children and he spoke soothingly to them.

Other teens helped corral the younger kids and entertain them while the adults worked on the wounded. Some of the adults in the community had served as emergency medical technicians before the

Troubles, or in hospitals as nurses or emergency room doctors. After the troubles, they made sure all the capable adults had training in field first aid.

"We sure work well together," Amy said.

"That we do," Paul agreed.

"We lost the Sanders family's vehicle," the elder said to the gathering after the wounded were tended. "We'll have to do what we can to get this family and their gear into some other cars." He looked at a notepad, then looked back up to the crowd. "If my information is correct, the Grossmans can take the two Sanders children."

Mr. Grossman waved his hand and nodded agreement.

They then figured out where the luggage would go and where the parents would ride. As it turned out the car behind the Grossmans had room for the parents.

"We were lucky," Elder Franklin said. "Our injuries were minor and will heal. The car can be replaced a little later. What we didn't anticipate was how desperate the gangs in Richmond are getting. The fact that they tried to ambush a large and well-armed caravan shows just how far down they have come. We thank God for His protection and love. Now, let's get that car's load redistributed and get out of here. We'll take a longer rest stop in about an hour."

Everyone got busy. The damaged car's load was moved to three other vehicles, some of it strapped to luggage racks. Within fifteen minutes the caravan was moving again.

FOUR

Base

THE TRIP FROM HOME to the capital used to take about five hours by car. This time it took most of the day. After Richmond, there were no more incidents. Paul noticed little activity in the towns they passed and as they drove into the metropolitan area of Washington, D. C., all they saw were abandoned buildings and cars. No traffic moved on the freeway or the surface streets.

The caravan rolled into Arlington and along Arlington Mill Drive to the Hilton Garden Inn. The city of Arlington was empty, as was the Hilton. Power and water service still worked, surprisingly, so they would make use of the abandoned hotel as a base of operations.

Randy again directed cars when they arrived at the hotel parking lot. A young married couple who led a singles' Bible study set up at the registration desk with lists. Families were assigned multiple room suites, while couples or singles got other rooms. There were more than enough. Key cards were simple enough to duplicate for access to the rooms, and the entire mission team got unloaded and into assigned rooms in short order.

Maid service, of course, was not available. Actually, the hotel was pretty dusty all over. It had been more than nine months since anyone had worked there. The first order of business once in the rooms was stripping the beds and getting the linen and other bedding into the hotel laundry facilities. For the first night or two, the members of the mission would use their own sleeping bags.

Everyone met in one of the larger conference rooms after check-in.

Members of the mission divided into groups that would rotate through various direct mission and support tasks. Laundry and cleaning were assigned to one group, meal preparation was assigned to another. Several small teams were assigned scouting into the district.

Two families, who also ran the church Sunday school, took over one of the large conference rooms in the hotel and brought in toys and materials. They had volunteered to handle all the child care, Bible school work while the older teens and adults worked on the other mission jobs.

Sheets of paper handed out during the meeting advised everyone to not leave the hotel at night, drink only bottled water, use stairs when practical since electric power could go out at any time, and not use the hotel swimming pool. The pool water was dark green and probably dangerous.

For the first evening, though, the mission would stand down, have a picnic dinner, and relax before the hard work began in the morning.

The Shannons and Grossmans joined each other for the evening picnic and found a place across the road along the stream.

Roger and Sarah ran through the tall grass, laughing and yelling. Occasionally they would return to the picnic blankets and eat something, then run off again. The parents reviewed the trip and the plans for the next couple of days. Paul's dad shifted position on the blanket to ease the pressure from the pistol poking into his back.

Paul and Amy sat close and talked softly. Paul could tell Amy was visibly shaken by the attempted ambush in Richmond. While no one in their cars was injured, a bullet had creased the roof of the Grossmans' car.

"I think my ears are still ringing from when Mom fired her pistol from the window," Paul said. "Man, that was loud."

"I can imagine," Amy said. "I just stayed down on the floor and prayed."

"Are you excited about going into the district tomorrow?" Paul asked.

"I kind of am. I'm sure we'll see some awful things, but I'm eager to help. Those poor people have been wandering around out there for so long, and after being immersed in that fog for days. Hard to believe anyone lived through that black fog."

"Yeah." Paul looked down at his now empty plate. "We both saw how awful it was for Joe, and he just got brushed by it. That tiny tendril of fog tortured him into unconsciousness. It had to be the most horrible thing. I think about it a lot. I wish I'd been able to help him."

Amy put her hand on Paul's, trying to comfort. Paul's Mom noticed and glanced away, smiling.

"We have a chance to help, now," Amy said.

#

The Shannon family spent the rest of the evening cleaning up their rooms. The months of dust accumulated on furniture and fixtures was not simply wiped away, but required a lot of extra work. Vacuums from the housekeeping rooms were brought around and used. Some cleaning fluids and other products helped get the rooms livable. Pags and towels were added to the laundry piles for the next day.

Paul got his sleeping bag unrolled on one of the beds. He then got his toothbrush and toothpaste and headed to the bathroom.

"You and Amy are pretty close," Mom said quietly, coming up behind him. "Are you getting to be more than friends?"

"Uh," Paul tried to respond. "She, uh …"

"It's all right, Paul. Amy is a wonderful Christian girl and you two are great friends. That makes for the foundation of a wonderful, life-long marriage."

"Marriage?"

"Don't worry, that's a long time coming." She put her arm around Paul's shoulders. "As much as you like Amy, and as good friends as you are, you must remember one thing, son. A strong relationship is built on respect for each other. You and Amy have that now, and with God's help, you can maintain it, let your love grow, and still wait for marriage."

Paul swallowed. "You're way ahead of me, Mom. I haven't even kissed her yet—or any girl, for that matter."

Mom squeezed his shoulder. "I know. But, it's wise to get ahead of these things. I love Amy, and if you chose her someday to be your wife, I would be very happy."

Paul felt his mouth drop open as he thought about what his mom had said. Then he realized that he could not imagine a future without Amy in it.

"Hmm," he finally said. "Yeah." He looked at his mother. "Mom, I promise I will always respect Amy and I will wait for marriage."

"Thank you," she said, and went off to her room.

Paul stood in front of the bathroom for a few minutes, letting this sink in. *I can't believe it,* he thought. *I just had a conversation with my mom about my future marriage.*

No, he couldn't image a future—his future—without Amy in it. But marriage? He wasn't ready to think about that yet. He went in and brushed his teeth.

#

The entire group had a light breakfast in the hotel restaurant. Those who were venturing into the district for the day picked up sack lunches from tables in the lobby marked with large signs labeled "AWAY" on the way out.

Paul looked at the sign a moment. Then a young man patted his shoulder.

"We're away teams," he said. "I'm Brad, and this is Janet, my wife. You and Amy are assigned to us for this first round."

They shook hands as Amy came up with her lunch. Brad and Janet, Paul knew, were active in the young married groups and small groups in the church. Brad was a tall, beefy, tough looking man and Janet was a tall, slender woman with long brown hair.

This day was mostly for scouting. They would identify any potential facility that could be used for housing, feeding and caring for black fog survivors. They would also note the location of any survivors they found.

Actual contact with survivors today was discouraged. The important thing was to note where they were and find an adequate facility. A school, preferably a high school, ought to have a gym, showers, and other resources to help with the mission.

They also needed to hunt down civil defense or emergency shelters where they could find nonperishable food, cots, blankets, and other supplies. These would be moved to the chosen facilities and used to help the survivors.

Paul and Amy brought their backpacks and staffs and picked up additional equipment, including binoculars, flashlights, latex gloves, and surgical-style face masks.

"You brought your sword, right?" Amy said while they were alone.

"Always," Paul said. He nodded toward Brad and Janet. "Guess we're ready."

"We're lucky," Brad said when Paul and Amy walked up. "We get to scout out the mall. We have the area from the Lincoln Memorial to RFK stadium on the east end. Lots of cool things to see!"

"It'll keep us busy," Janet said, tying her hair back. "That's for sure."

"We're all ready," Amy said.

They climbed into Brad and Janet's green Crossover and drove off. Brad got on the freeway. There were no other vehicles to be seen except for wrecked and abandoned cars.

"Hard to believe people used to complain about traffic," Janet said.

They exited at the Pentagon, then drove past Arlington Cemetery and across Arlington Memorial Bridge. Brad pulled the vehicle around to the front of the Lincoln Memorial and stopped.

The first thing Paul noticed after getting out of the car was a sour note to the air. It just didn't have a "fresh" feel to it. Judging by the looks on their faces, the others noticed it too.

They'd all brought binoculars. They used these now to scan the area. Paul was first to call out that he saw a survivor.

"There's a ... person, right over there," Paul said, pointing toward a sidewalk leading to the Vietnam Veterans Memorial. He couldn't tell if it was a man or a woman. Through the binoculars, Paul could see matted hair hanging around the shoulders. The survivor's body was thin and the face was hollow-eyed and emaciated. The clothing so soiled it was uniformly black and sagging. The person stood still for a moment, took a step or two, then stopped and just stood looking around.

Then the survivor turned to face Paul and looked directly at him. A shiver went down Paul's spine at the sight of the blank eyes fixed on him. A moment later, the survivor turned and looked at Amy.

After that, the survivor turned away and took a few more slow, plodding steps the other direction.

Paul lowered his binoculars and exchanged glances with Amy.

"That was weird," she said.

"Paul, make a note of this survivor," said Brad. "Just the location. We'll keep our distance for now."

Paul complied, noting the location of the survivor. They spent a few more minutes scanning the area and identified a few more survivors. The other survivors ignored them. The only one to pay any attention to them, that Paul could tell, was that first one. Paul watched another one that moved about ten feet down the walk to the Korean War Veterans Memorial, turned and walked the ten feet back, then turned and repeated the process. From this distance and through the binoculars, Paul could see a darkened smear along the path the survivor walked.

"They're lost," he said to no one in particular. "Not just lost about where they are, but lost in their souls."

Brad came up after looking around by the Reflecting Pond.

"We'll drive along the pond, here, over in the grass. I want to stay out in the open, away from the buildings for now. We'll go slow and stop when you see someone. Once you note the location, we'll move on. Okay?"

"It's a plan," Paul said.

Brad drove his Crossover over the curb and across a small plaza to the south side of the pond. He drove slowly out into the open grass. The going was smooth enough and they were able to scan with the binoculars along the tree-lined walks. Amy called out and they stopped while she recorded a survivor on her notepad.

"Okay," she said, and they moved on.

FIVE

Recon

THEY CONTINUED DOWN the mall, past the Word War II Memorial toward the Washington Monument. Someone would call out and they would stop for a moment. Paul noticed that most of the survivors would look at them—often directly at him or Amy—and then ignore them. Other than that, the survivors had no interest in any of them.

"I can see the White House!" Amy said. Paul looked across and nodded.

"Bet we could get a tour today." He grinned.

"We'll be running down F Street and Pennsylvania Avenue tomorrow," Brad said. "Might be a good time to do a recon of the White House."

Amy smiled broadly, barely containing her excitement.

"I'd love to!" she said.

"Me, too," Janet said. "I've always wanted to see the inside."

Brad continued driving and navigated around the Washington Monument, then down the center of the mall between the grand museums and the Smithsonian Institute. A few more survivors were spotted and recorded. They seemed to be randomly scattered and didn't cluster together in any way.

One survivor they saw was near a door to the Hirshhorn Museum, a large, round, multi-storied donut of a building. The survivor would walk up to the door, push on it, then turn and walk away. Then the survivor turned and walked back up to the door. They observed this for a few iterations.

"The fog came right in the middle of their lives," Paul speculated. "What we're seeing must be what they were doing just about the time the fog arrived. They seem to be on some kind of endless loop, replaying that activity."

"Interesting idea," Brad said. "It might help us identify who some of those people might be when we get them to a shelter."

After a few more sightings, Brad drove around the Capitol Reflecting Pool and in front of the Capitol Building. He stopped and got out, digging out some papers from his pack.

"One of our other tasks is to find emergency stores," he said as the others gathered around. He unfolded a map on the hood. "There's an underground passage from the Capitol to the office building, over there." He pointed to the map, then pointed to the office building visible just north and behind the Capitol. "There is another to the south. Those office buildings have emergency stores in their lower floors. We need to see if the emergency stores are still there, and assess their condition."

Paul was suddenly creeped out by the thought of going into a tunnel. He shivered.

Brad looked at him and chuckled.

"This is the only place we'll be doing this today, Paul," he said. "We're all going together. We'll also use the latex gloves and face masks. Don't touch anything in here with bare skin."

"Okay," Paul said, and breathed deeply.

"Look," Janet said. She pointed to the south stairs on the Capitol. A survivor, wearing what looked like the remains of a nice suit and carrying a brief case, was slowly coming down the stairs. As they looked, the survivor stopped, turned and started back up.

"I'll bet that's someone we want to get right away," she said. She wrote down the location of the survivor. "This one may be a former representative."

"Good catch," Brad said.

They watched the lost soul for a moment. The survivor turned briefly and looked at them, then continued its routine.

"How do we get into this tunnel?" Amy said, shifting everyone's attention.

"We go in here," Brad said, pointing to the map, "then down some stairs over here, and into the tunnels. The shuttles probably aren't running under there, but we can make the walk."

"Let's go, then," Paul said. "Let's get this done."

Everyone put on protective gear, then Brad locked the vehicle. Amy laughed at that.

"Not much chance the survivors will try to steal the car," she said.

Paul shrugged. "We still don't know what else may be around. Best to be careful."

In the Capitol Building, they found the stairs on the Senate side leading to the tunnel. Paul reached up his right hand and checked his sword in the backpack. It was there and a comfort.

They weren't quiet going into the stairwell, with Amy's and Paul's staffs clacking on the floor tiles. So far, the survivors didn't seem to be bothered by or attracted to sounds. They just kept to their endless loop behavior. Paul was relieved they did not encounter any more survivors.

The tunnel was a beige tiled nightmare, dimly lit with poor visibility. A thick layer of dust coated everything. In a way, Paul thought, that was good. There were no other footprints in the dust. On the left was a track for the shuttles that would ferry senators from the offices to the Capitol. The dust was thick there, too.

"Go easy," Brad said. "Let's not kick up too much dust. These masks are only so good."

In spite of the lack of other footprints, they moved slowly and Brad led with a flashlight. The light wasn't strictly necessary—there was enough filtered sunlight to show the way—but the little beam did make the place feel less gloomy.

Dust still puffed up as they walked and the masks became more difficult to breathe through. Finally they came to the end of the tunnel and climbed into the office building. They stopped and replaced the masks with fresh ones. The office building was just as dusty as the tunnel, but a bit more brightly lit with sunlight streaming through dirty windows.

No other tracks were visible on the floor or down the halls.

"We're good so far," Brad said, his voice puffing and animating his mask. "Now we go across to another stairwell. That leads down to the emergency supplies lockers."

He led the way down a hall and across the building. There were still no other footprints to be seen, and the door to the next stairwell was closed. They opened the door and found the stairwell dark. A light switch just inside did not turn on any lights.

"Broken or burned out," Brad said.

They all got their flashlights going and proceeded down the stairs. The dust on the stairs was undisturbed. At the bottom, Brad led them down a short hall and through another door. This opened into a large storeroom lined with metal cages. Pallets inside the cages held piles of boxes, bags, and bins. The flashlights revealed the labels on the emergency stores they sought.

Janet, back at the door, flipped a switch. Lights flickered on, giving the room some illumination. "Let's get a bit of an inventory," Brad said. He pulled a crowbar from his pack and broke the hasp that locked the first cage. "Paul, Amy, have at this one."

He continued down the line of cages. Janet went into the next one and they could hear Brad breaking hasps. The first cage held mostly food, it appeared to Paul. The pallets kept the bags and boxes dry and off the concrete floor. That would insure the foodstuffs would not spoil. He and Amy listed a pallet of rice bags, a pallet of wheat flour, and a pallet each of canned beans, peas, corn, string beans, and tomatoes. The palleted supplies were all wrapped in plastic and seemed untouched.

Amy inspected one of the boxes of canned corn through the plastic. "The date here says the corn is still good for four more years," she said. "It's kind of like being in a Costco."

They finished with that cage, then leapfrogged down the room to the next one beyond Brad. This cage contained medical supplies. Everything was packaged and carefully sealed in plastic containers. They found surgical instruments, topical antibiotics, bandages, surgical barriers, and clothing. "Everything you need for a field hospital," Paul said. He noted autoclaves, and small generators, lamps, and other equipment all, wrapped and sterile.

In the next cage, Paul and Amy stopped short. There were racks of pistols, rifles, and other arms. Pallets of ammunition were stacked alongside the racks of weapons. Most of the weapons were coated with a greasy substance and all the racks were vacuum-sealed in plastic.

"This could turn our mission into a small army," he said. He counted the number of rifles, pistols, shotguns, and small rocket launchers.

"Is that grease all over the guns?" Amy said.

"Cosmoline. It keeps the guns from rusting. When it's packed air-tight like this, you can take these out, wipe them off with a rag, and use them."

"There are a lot of them."

"I count a hundred and fifty rifles, an equal number of pistols, forty-five shotguns and twenty rocket launchers. What's weird is that these aren't in an arms locker, better secured. Look how easily we got to them."

Brad poked his head into the cage. "Wow!" he said. "My last cage was all shovels and bags of concrete and such."

"We'll want to get this cache secured at the mission base," Paul said. "Never know if we'll need it."

"Right." Brad's eyes surveyed the racks of rifles. "M-27s. Also known as IARs. I used them in the military. Weird that they aren't better secured. Good find, Paul."

"You used those?"

"Yeah," Brad said. "Marine grunt. Afghanistan."

SIX

Facility

BACK AT THE CAR, the team pulled off the latex gloves and brushed themselves off before climbing in. Brad made notes on the location and on the more direct access route to the storage room through the office building. They came back through the tunnel to keep their tracks in one place and not expose their presence in the office building. Tomorrow, a truck and crew would follow Brad's directions to start gathering the supplies.

"Now we continue down East Capitol Street," said Brad. "We'll stay in the street and record any survivors we see. Our next task is to assess the high school on the east end. We'll eat lunch soon, then scout the school and RFK Stadium. Then we head back to the hotel."

They rolled slowly and found a few survivors shambling among the residential buildings lining the street. One tried to get into a car, then turned back to the house. When they stopped to record this one, the survivor turned and looked at Paul, then went back to the endless loop between the car and the house.

Brad bumped over the curb at Lincoln Park and drove through the plaza. No survivors were there, so he stopped.

"Lunch," he said. He passed around hand sanitizer, and they all dug into their sacks.

"It's weird that we don't see anyone inside buildings, only outside," Amy said between bites of her sandwich. "We didn't see any sign of anyone inside the Capitol or the office building. I haven't seen any movement behind windows in these row houses. Why are the only survivors we've seen outside?"

"Good questions," Janet said. "I've looked through windows, too, with the binoculars. No movement, nothing."

"Yeah," Brad said. "And as dirty as the survivors are, they're hard to spot out in the open unless they move."

Brad looked around the park. The only other human-like thing around was the statue of Mary McLeod Bethune across an overgrown grassy patch.

Amy saw him looking at the statue. "She was an educator and civil rights advocate. She even served as an advisor to President Roosevelt. In the forties."

"You a little mobile encyclopedia?" Brad asked, raising his eyebrows.

Amy blushed. "Just a little snippet."

"Oh, she'll surprise you with those, sometimes," Paul said. Amy punched his arm.

They finished eating and cleaned up the lunch trash. Janet stuffed it into a plastic bag and tossed it into the back of the Chevy. Then Brad started the car, bumped up some stairs, and drove across the grassy patch and around the statue.

As before, they rolled slowly down the street and recorded another handful of survivors. At Seventeenth Street, they found the high school.

"Let's pull around the back side by the football field," Brad said as he turned north on Seventeeth. "I think we'll probably work from that side."

A narrow lane and parking spaces made up A Street between the high school building and the football field. On the east side of the campus was the gymnasium. Brad stopped near it.

"Check around for any survivors nearby," he said, getting out.

Paul spotted a survivor near the DC Armory with his binoculars. Amy picked up one on the far side of a parking lot toward RFK Stadium. No one saw any other survivors nearby.

"Masks and latex again?" Paul said.

"Got it," Brad said. "Let's see how things look in here."

They geared up and headed toward the entrance to the gym. The doors were not locked, so they carefully opened them and looked inside. No lights were on. The dust was undisturbed.

As before, they walked carefully and tried not to stir up too much dust. By the time they'd looked through the bulk of the school building and noted the location of large rooms, their masks were dust-clogged and dust covered the rest of their faces. The clogged masks became more and more difficult to breath through. Sweat trailed through the dust coating their faces and itched. When they itched or rubbed, it smeared and made it worse.

Brad looked through the locker and showers and pronounced them more than adequate for processing the survivors. The pull-out bleachers in the gym would not be needed, but there were a lot of folding tables and chairs in storage rooms nearby that could be used for eating and work areas.

The nurse's station was small but could function as a triage area. They would need to set up a larger clinic area nearby. Paul suggested one of the classrooms next door be tagged for that purpose.

At the car, they stripped off the latex and masks, and breathed deeply. Janet passed around wet wipes and they cleaned off their faces as best they could.

"This is an excellent location for a processing center," Brad said. He grabbed a can of red spray paint and painted a large red check mark on the doors to the gym, then placed a small stick in front of the doors. If someone came before their crews showed up, this would give them a warning.

"I don't know if there is anyone else, or anything else, here," Brad said. "But we should always assume the worst until something shows us different." He gathered their used latex and masks and put them in a plastic bag, then tossed that into the back of the Chevy.

"So RFK Stadium is next?" Paul asked.

"Short trip. I don't think we need to do much besides check for survivors there. Note any resources we can use. That kind of thing."

"Good," Amy said. "I'm about ready to head back."

RFK Stadium, the former home of the Washington Redskins, had hosted the Washington Nationals baseball team and the DC United soccer team until the Troubles. As a multi-use facility, it was also a venue for concerts and other community events. Most access points were locked and chained. From what the team could see, there were no survivors inside. There were a few false alarms when some movement in the stairs or ramps brought them up short, but it always turned out to be blowing trash and not survivors.

They made a complete circuit of the stadium and found no easy access.

"Well, we can come back to this if we need a larger facility," Brad said. "As it stands, we really can't make much use of it since it it's an open stadium. Not covered. But the locks won't prevent us from getting in later with the right tools."

He made notes and they all got back into the car.

"To the Hilton, please," Amy said.

#

The teams gathered in the large conference room as they returned and shared the information. Survivors were scattered throughout the city, alone, lost, and repeating a sequence of actions over and over, just as Paul and Amy's team observed. The main difference was that none of the other teams reported survivors who looked at them or paid any attention to them at all.

Two more schools were selected and marked for use in housing and working with the survivors. A couple of other emergency supply caches were discovered as well, but none had weapons as the one in the Senate Office Building did. Another team would check out the House Office Building tomorrow.

Another group reported they had found several trucks in former rental businesses and said they would bring those around to the supply caches to transport material to the selected school sites. Others would be taking cleaning equipment to each of the schools to clean up the sites and make them ready.

Surgical gowns and barrier clothing were found in sufficient quantities at a nearby hospital. The teams that would make contact and try to recover the survivors would wear full sets of surgical barrier garb.

"This should help prevent the spread of any diseases or infections," the woman who provided the report said. "Direct physical contact with the survivors should be avoided until we get them cleaned up."

A man next to the woman spoke up. "In addition, you'll all get a bottle of mentholated cream. We recommend you smear a generous amount of this inside your face masks before gathering or working with any of the survivors. It'll help mask the smell. Individually, they'll smell bad enough. When we get a bunch of them together, it'll be overwhelming."

"How do you know this works?" someone in the audience asked.

"I'm a police officer," he said, holding up a small glass bottle of mentholated cream. "We keep this in our cars for when we respond to reports of someone possibly dead for several days. It works."

Paul and Amy looked at each other, eyes wide.

"This is going to be awful for a few days," Paul whispered to her. "Glad to know this trick."

"We never got close enough to smell anything," she whispered back. "It must be bad."

"Didn't you notice the kind of sour smell in the air when we got into town? I think that might be from the survivors."

"Oh, gross."

"Yeah."

#

Paul walked across the hotel lobby with plans to get some sleep in his room. In one of the side rooms, he saw a man working on something at a table. He knew of this guy; his name was James Carson. He was one of the new people who had started coming to church after the Troubles. All that upheaval had caused a lot of people to turn to God, or to return to Him. Paul hand't spoken much with James, but they'd been introduced.

What's he working on? Paul asked himself.

"Hi," Paul said as he entered the small side room. Then he stopped. On the table in front of James was an arm and a leg, and he was trying to adjust something on the arm using some small tools—and just one hand.

"Hi, Paul," James said. Then he stiffened and grimaced in pain.

"Are you okay?" Paul asked coming to the table.

After a couple seconds, James relaxed and nodded. "Yeah, I'm okay. Just tired and need to get my TENS treatment."

"Can I help?"

James sighed and looked down a moment. Then he looked up at Paul with a weary smile. "Sure. Sometimes, I just have to give it to Jesus and let others help." He handed Paul a small wrench, then pointed to a spot near the elbow of the prosthetic arm. "I need to tighten that nut, but it's almost impossible to do with just one hand. Don't know who designed these things, but I'd like to have a long talk with him or her."

Paul manipulated the small wrench and tightened the nut.

"Just a little tight," James said. "It still has to move."

"How's that?" Paul asked. He flexed the arm a little to show that it still bent.

"Excellent. Thank you."

"I didn't realize you were missing an arm … uh … and a leg," Paul said.

"Well, there are times—" he paused as he stiffened again and pain reflected on his face—"when my body refuses to accept that parts are missing." He rubbed his left shoulder.

"What do you mean?"

"It's called phantom limb syndrome," James said. "The body gets phantom pain and cramps that it thinks are coming from the missing parts. It comes and goes. Over time, it's supposed to happen less. I'm still waiting."

"I'm not sure what to say," Paul said. "What's a tense treatment?"

"A TENS. That's an electronic pulse that helps ease the inflamed nerves. It helps when I can get to power or get the unit charged." He looked at his watched. "And I take some pain relievers, too." He retrieved a small bottle from his pocket, shook out two tabs, and popped them in his mouth. He chased that with a sip of water from a bottle on the table. "I'm not sure what I'll do when we can't find any more of this stuff, or it all expires."

"Can I ask how …" Paul stopped and looked down. "I'm sorry, I don't mean to pry."

"It's okay, Paul. I lost my arm and leg to an improvised explosive device in Iraq. I'm the lucky one. My battalion commander, my staff sergeant, and several others in the battalion HQ didn't make it."

"Can I pray for you?"

"Sure." James smiled. "I've been prayed over a lot in the last few years. My faith has been sorely tested, but I think it all helps."

Guy L. Pace

SEVEN

White House

THE NEXT MORNING dawned bright and sunny. Paul and Amy joined Brad and Janet at the car after breakfast, geared up and ready for another day.

"Why do you guys bring those sticks with you everywhere?" Janet asked as they put their gear into the car.

"We depended on them a lot during the Troubles," Amy said. "And the bo is my favorite weapon in martial arts."

"The bo?" Janet said raising her eyebrows.

"It's the Japanese word for staff, or stick. These are a more beat-up version of what I train with."

"They are pretty scarred up," Brad noted.

"They got a lot of use," Paul said.

They headed into the city, crossed the Theodore Roosevelt Memorial Bridge, turned north, and pulled over on F Street.

"The routine today," Brad said, "is similar to yesterday. We're going to locate survivors and record their locations and any other things we see. We also have a couple buildings to check for supply caches. The White House is one of those."

"Sounds better, actually," Amy said, smiling. "I get to see the inside of the White House!"

"I hope you're not too disappointed," Janet said. "It hasn't been maintained or cleaned for a long time."

"I couldn't be disappointed," Amy said. "I can look past the dust."

Paul scanned the area around them with his binoculars. Virginia Avenue slashed diagonally northwest to southeast behind them, crossing Twenty-Third Street NW. A survivor shambled back and forth in front of the Ivory Tower, a George Washington University structure on the northwest corner of the intersection.

Across Virginia Avenue to the south, Paul saw a dark pile on the sidewalk. The slight breeze fluttered some of the cloth in the pile.

"Brad, look," he said, pointing. "We should check this out."

Brad brought up his binoculars. "Looks like clothing. We just drove past it coming up. I didn't notice then. Yeah, let's take a look. Carefully."

They spread out and walked slowly across the intersection. Paul, on the right, viewed the survivor on the north side. The survivor looked directly at Paul, then turned back to its repetitive activity.

Paul shivered, then checked the area around the pile he'd seen. He didn't see any other survivors nearby. As they got closer, Paul noticed something: dark spots on the pavement. When he got to them, he bent down to take a closer look. The pavement looked burned in the shape of a large paw print, about as wide across as the distance between Paul's outstretched thumb and little finger. A sulfurous, burnt smell came from it. Scorch marks spread from the print, as if someone had used a blow torch to craft it. The print was one of many that lead to the pile on the sidewalk, and they all came from the northwest up Virginia Avenue.

He looked up at the others.

"Something came through here," he said. "Something big."

Brad, closer to the pile, covered his nose and mouth with his hand and nodded. Both Amy and Janet moved away from the pile. After a moment of study, Brad moved away from the pile, as well.

"Well," Brad said when he uncovered his nose and mouth, "that was once a survivor. Those tracks lead right up to it. Looks like the survivor was eaten. Mostly."

"The tracks continue to the north from here," Amy said.

Those aren't normal tracks, Paul thought. *Whatever made them is huge, and hot. Hot enough to burn an impression into a road surface just by walking on it.*

Paul went back to the car and got his tablet out of his backpack. It had a camera in it. He came back and took a few pictures of the tracks and the pile, as close as he could stand to get.

He showed the pictures to the others.

"Now we know why we're getting mentholated cream," he said. "Those remains smelled horrible. I hope I can get that out of my nose."

They all nodded agreement and headed back to the car.

On the way back, the survivor on the northwest corner looked at Paul and Amy again. It stared for a moment, then turned back to its cycle of movement.

Paul stopped in the middle of the intersection and grabbed Brad's arm. "That was the first time a survivor looked at me more than once. Not only that, it actually stared for a moment."

"Are you sure?"

"Yes," Paul said. "It looked at Amy, too. The first time it looked at me was when we went to the body. Then just now it looked again."

Brad looked around on the street and found some small stones. He picked them up and set himself to toss one. "We'll see if this gets its attention." As the survivor shuffled away from them, Brad tossed the stone at it. It bounced on the sidewalk near the survivor's feet. The survivor didn't flinch or pay any attention to the stone. Brad dropped the other one.

"Well, that should have had some response," he said.

"Let's move on, then," Paul said. "This is starting to freak me out."

They got in the car and drove slowly down F Street. They recorded several survivors over the few blocks before they came to Seventeeth Street SW. Brad turned the car north and they drove slowly up to Pennsylvania Avenue and came around the Eisenhower Executive Office Building. A couple more survivors were spotted, and then they found two more right in front of the White House, near the west gate.

Brad turned south down Executive Avenue.

"Good thing we're the only ones around," he said. "I'm going the wrong way on a one-way here." He pulled up to the gate of the West Wing.

Amy was beside herself with excitement as they got out.

"Latex and masks again," Brad said. "We don't know what we're going to find here. Let's be prepared."

Paul made a sweep of the area with his binoculars while they were getting latex gloves and masks on. He didn't see any survivors other than the ones on Pennsylvania Avenue.

They made their way through the gate and moved up to the West Wing. A bit of trash tumbled across the North Lawn, pushed along by the light breeze. Amy may have been excited, but the rest of the team was jumpy. Paul and Brad both made double-takes at the trash when it moved.

The doors and windows they could see were intact and the doors weren't locked. They couldn't see any fresh tracks of any kind outside and none in the dust inside. They went inside.

A patina of dust coated everything. Desks in the adjacent offices had loose paper on them and spilling to the floor. Everything looked like people just got up and left, or evaporated from their chairs in the middle of the day.

Down a short hall, they entered the main lobby. A door to the right took them into a hall with offices on the right for the Vice President and the Chief of Staff office. The hall turned left and brought them to the Oval Office on the right and the Roosevelt Room on the left. The hall continued to the left. Down there was the Cabinet Room and around to the right was the Press Briefing Room along the West Colonnade.

Amy opened the door to the Oval Office and went in. Paul followed. Brad and Janet checked out the Roosevelt Room.

"Wow!" Amy said walking around the large desk. She turned and took in the whole room. "I've always wanted to see this room. It really is oval!"

She looked out the grimy windows into the untended, overgrown, weedy Rose Garden. "This must have been beautiful in the summer, with the roses in bloom and everything cared for and tended."

"Kinda sad, now," Paul said.

"Yeah."

"We need to go check out the Situation Room," Paul said. "Let's get back with Brad and Janet."

They left the Oval Office, met the others, and followed Brad down to the Situation Room. They checked in and around it and found nothing they could use for supplies.

"The other place that would probably have something will be the President's Emergency Operations Center, over under the East Wing," Brad said. He lead them back up and across to the residence.

As they moved through the ground floor of the residence, they checked entry doors for evidence of entry and tracks. All the windows appeared to be closed, with no evidence of entry or disturbed dust. The Center Hall took them to the Visitor's Foyer at the East Colonnade. They navigated to the East Wing and down into the President's Emergency Operations Center, the PEOC.

Paul noted the thick concrete as they passed into the PEOC.

"It's a bunker," Brad said, noting Paul's interest in the concrete. "It was built to withstand anything but a direct hit by a nuclear ICBM. There should be emergency rations, supplies, and other tools down here."

Janet found a door in the far end of the room and went in. "Found it!"

Inside was a kitchen down one side, and racks of food, medical supplies, and other material supplies down the other. They all went to work getting an inventory of the contents of the room.

"Looks like you could keep some folks alive in here for a long time," Paul said as he wrote down lists of food. "There's not as much as in the Senate Office Building, but it's still quite a bit."

EIGHT

Union Station

WHEN THEY FINISHED up in the PEOC, Paul accompanied Amy through the rest of the White House. Then they met back at the car, outside the West Wing. During the tour of the upstairs of the residence, Paul saw a survivor wandering around the pond on the South Lawn. He recorded that and reported it to Brad when he returned to the car.

They got back in the car and Brad drove south, around the President's Park, and back north on Fifteenth Street NW, to F Street. He pointed out the Treasury Building as they turned east.

He drove slowly down F Street, but they could see ahead for blocks the few survivors along the sidewalks in front of the tall buildings lining the street. As they passed cross streets, Brad slowed more so they could scan north and south.

By the time they reached Judiciary Square, they'd recorded fifteen more survivors. They pulled over to the curb on the north side of the square and got out their sack lunches.

"So how did you like the White House?" Janet asked Amy.

"It was sad," she said. "So dusty and neglected now. The gardens are all overgrown and weedy. The huge lawns are brown and the grass hasn't been maintained. Some of the rooms there, it seemed as if people just stood and left and never came back. Things were left where they were set down on desks and tables. Trash cans still had trash in them. It was just sad. I hope we can bring the government back here someday so we can get this city back to what it should be."

"Our work here may help," Brad said. He glanced at Paul, then back to Janet. "Assuming we don't find more than just survivors."

Paul finished off his sandwich and peeled his banana. "I think there will be a lot of cleanup to do, depending on how long they wait. I'm getting out to stretch a bit."

He walked around the car a couple times. The others got out as well. Paul pointed to the building across the street to the north.

"Look, The National Building Museum," he said. "A building that's a museum about buildings."

Amy looked at the building, then laughed and continued laughing. The laughter turned into giggles and she leaned on Paul's shoulder. Soon, she was taking deep breaths.

"Sorry," she said between gasps, "that just struck me strangely."

"It's okay," Paul said, his arm around her shoulders. "We need some tension relief."

"Well, if everyone is done stretching and giggling," Brad said, "we need to move on. We're going to take a turn and go south to E Street, then head east to Union Station."

They all climbed in the car and Brad drove to Fourth Street NW and turned south. At E Street, he turned east and they slowly crossed the overpass at Interstate 395. They kept moving slowly and recording survivors they saw, then they were in front of Union Station.

Paul tried to get a quick count of the number of survivors widely scattered around the front of the former transportation hub of the city. He thought there were about twenty.

"I see some piles," Paul said, "like we found by Virginia Avenue."

"Can we get close to them without getting close to any of the active survivors?" Brad asked.

"Yeah, those two over there." Paul pointed to the junction of Delaware Avenue and Columbus Circle. The street was actually an arc that curved around the front of the station. "They're far enough from the active ones."

Brad left the car where E Street dumped into Columbus Circle. Paul got out, grabbing his tablet. Amy and Janet followed, keeping a close eye on the moving survivors.

One of the piles was on the sidewalk on the west corner of the Delaware Avenue junction. The other was in the traffic island between the one-way lanes of Columbus Circle, just across the street.

They crossed Louisiana Avenue and slowly approached the pile. As before, it turned out to be the remains of a survivor that appeared to have been eaten. The same burned tracks, wide as Paul could stretch his hand across, led to the remains, and then returned in the direction of the station.

Paul took pictures with the tablet. When he compared them to the ones before, these pictures showed the tracks to be less distinct, more gray.

"I think these tracks are older," he told Brad. "See how they aren't as sharp and distinct?"

Brad looked and nodded. "Let's check the other one."

They crossed the street to the other remains. Amy nudged Paul and pointed at some of the active survivors. Several nearby had stopped and were intently watching Paul and Amy.

Bones and clothing were all that were left of the survivor that was in this location. The same tracks were there. They were less distinct, indicating the same age, coming from and returning to the station.

The survivors Amy pointed out were still watching them. They weren't moving, just watching.

"The smell is getting to me," Paul said after taking more pictures. "Can we get out of here?"

"Yeah, let's go," Brad said. "This is getting weird, all those survivors watching you two."

They headed more directly back to the car and got in.

Brad turned in the driver's seat as Paul put the tablet away.

"I'm turning around so we can go a different route to Constitution Avenue and then head to the high school. We'll check on how things are going there, then head back to the hotel."

Amy and Paul nodded.

"Something about these survivors noticing you two," Janet said, "it's getting stronger or weirder."

"Stronger and weirder," Paul said.

"Creeps me out," Amy said.

Brad started the car, turned it around, and headed south. He took Louisiana Avenue to New Jersey Avenue, then turned east on

Constitution Avenue. When they got to Seventeenth Street, he turned south and then east into the parking area behind the high school gym.

Several vehicles and some trucks were there and the doors to the gym were wide open. Paul looked east, across the large parking lot and saw the survivor he'd spotted yesterday. It was still moving back and forth.

"With all the activity here today, you'd think it would change the survivor's activity," Paul said. "Seems they would be curious or interested. They just keep shuffling back and forth like zombies."

They got out of the car and went into the gym.

The floor shone and the dust was gone. Tables were set up along one side and cots were arranged across the floor. Blankets and pillows were on the cots.

Paul saw a woman he knew, Hazel Samson, busy making coffee. He remembered her bringing food for the family when Sarah and Roger were born. She ran that mission for the church and he wished he knew where she got all that energy and food. She seemed to have an endless supply of both. He went to her and spoke with her briefly and helped her arrange snacks at one of the tables.

"Looks like this is just about ready," Brad said.

Hazel looked up.

"Yes, we're almost done," she said. "We have the showers all cleaned out and running, and the clinic is all set up next to the nurse's station."

"We're done with our recon," Brad said, "so we'll be heading back to the hotel in a minute."

"Most of us here will be going back shortly, too," Hazel said. "We're just going to leave a small crew to keep an eye on things tonight."

A man walked into the gym just then.

"I'll stay here tonight with two others," he said, then held out his hand. "I'm Gary."

"I'm Brad." Brad took the offered hand. "Uh, Gary," Brad spoke in low tones, "we found some things today. May mean some wild animals out hunting. I strongly suggest that you lock and chain the doors when everyone else leaves for the night. Don't go out there."

Gary looked at Brad, then Amy, Paul and Janet.

"I'll make certain," he said.

"Good. Looks like you guys did a great job."

"Thanks."

Brad turned and led his crew back to the car.

#

At the hotel, they shared their information with the other recon teams. None reported any survivors paying any attention to them, but all had seen human remains at some locations. Those who had cameras or tablets had taken pictures of the remains and the tracks, as Paul had. Some of the tracks seemed fresh, with bold, black, burned areas. Others were faint, washed out, and hard to see except for the imprint in the blacktop or concrete. They were all huge and looked like large canine tracks.

"What's making those tracks?" one of the recon team members asked. "What's eating those survivors?"

"Good questions," Elder Franklin said coming in the door. "I overheard some of the reports. Could I see the pictures?"

He looked over the pictures and listened to what the others had seen.

Paul took a deep breath. "Elder Franklin, sometimes the survivors look at Amy and me. Today, they actually stared at us, a whole group of them at once."

Everyone looked at Paul. Amy, sitting near him, moved closer.

"I've seen it," Brad said. "I can tell, they look straight at Paul or Amy. Most of the time they only look for a moment, then turn back to their routine. Today, at Union Station, several of them just stopped and stared, just like Paul said."

"How big a group?" asked Elder Franklin.

"I counted about twenty-five active survivors in front of Union Station," Paul said. "Several more are ... no longer active."

"Wow!" said one of the other men. "We never saw more than one per block or so."

"Yeah," Paul said. "That was our experience, until Union Station."

"Well," Amy said, "there were five or so right around the White House."

"Right," Paul said.

"Come to think of it," a woman said, "we saw four or five right in the Washington Circle Park today. There were a couple of piles of remains just north of there. The tracks we saw led back toward Foggy Bottom."

Elder Franklin scratched his white head and thought.

"I don't like this," he said. "Tomorrow, we start rounding up some of these survivors. We have two facilities set up to take them in and clean them up. The pastor teams will be staying out there to work on the survivors we bring in.

"The adults in the recon and roundup team" —he looked around the room— "all of you need to start carrying pistols. If you don't have one, let me or one of the other leaders know. We now have quite a few."

Elder Franklin smiled and looked at Brad and his team.

#

"Are you okay?" Paul asked when he and Amy found a quiet place to talk after dinner.

"Yeah, just stressed," she said. "Thanks."

"Nothing to thank me for."

"Yes, there is. Being my friend and caring. Sorry for cracking up at the building museum."

"You didn't crack up," Paul said. "It is all kind of insane. Like last year, in a way. But we're not alone this time."

"You don't have to carry the huge burden alone this time." She watched Paul's face for a moment.

"But I get the feeling we're still in the middle of things."

"It sure looks that way."

They sat in silence until Amy said, "I'd better get to bed. We'll have a big day tomorrow."

"I'll walk you to your room," Paul said.

They found the stairs and worked their way up. At Amy's floor landing, she stopped at the door and looked at Paul.

"You're strong, Paul. I trust you." She leaned forward and kissed him on the cheek, then disappeared through the door.

Paul stood there for a few moments, his hand on his cheek. He felt flushed…and confused.

NINE

Gathering

AS THEY LEFT breakfast, Paul and Amy collected bundles of surgical barrier clothing in their general sizes.

"You have three sets in the bundle," the man handing out the gear said. "When they get dirty, strip them off, pack them in a plastic bag, and put on a fresh set."

"How dirty can they get?" Amy asked.

"You'll be working with the survivors today," he said. "Believe me, the barrier clothing will get very dirty."

When they got to the parking lot, Brad and Janet were waiting by the car.

"We head to the high school first," Brad said. "We join a truck team then and start gathering survivors."

Janet pointed at their staffs. "Good tool to have today," she said.

They all climbed into Brad's Chevy and Brad took the freeway on a swing through the south side of town, getting off at Potomac Avenue. He took that northeast to Seventeenth, then turned north. They were at the high school as other teams arrived and the doors were being unlocked and unchained.

Gary was waiting for them.

"The truck teams will be here in a few minutes," he said. "Come on in and relax for a few. We have coffee on."

Brad asked Gary if there had been any activity around the school the night before.

"No," he said. "I took your advice and chained everything up. We were snug and tight in here. Didn't hear a thing."

"Good."

Paul looked at the sky. This was the first gray morning since they'd arrived, and it looked like it might rain.

"I think we'll get wet today," he said. "How's this surgical stuff going to hold up when it rains?"

"We'll find out," Brad said. "Good thing they sent three sets."

Brad sipped at a cup of coffee, then nodded to a couple of trucks pulling up.

"This is how we're transporting the survivors."

They were larger, three-quarter ton trucks, with flat, stake-side beds. Benches had been fitted on the flat beds and steps flipped down in back to help the survivors get up into it.

"Even with the survivors in the flatbed," Brad said, "those guys driving the truck will have to deal with the smell. Hope they got extra bottles of the cream."

"How's this going to work?" Paul asked. "We aren't going to ride in back of the truck with the survivors, are we?"

"No," Brad said. "We follow in the car. We'll herd the survivors into the flatbed as we find them. The guys in the truck will put the gate and steps up and down and keep tabs on them."

"The guy who gave us the surgical gear said we'd get dirty," Amy said.

"Well, you don't want to touch the survivors, I don't think," Janet said. "But if you do, you probably ought to change the gear. Rain may complicate things."

"If you get a lot of smell on you," Brad said, "you change before you get back in the car."

They all opened their bundles and put on the surgical barrier clothing, including booties, latex gloves, and hoods. They smeared generous amounts of the mentholated cream inside their face masks. Paul put his mask on, then immediately pulled it down.

"Whew!" he said. "I think I'll put that on when we get there. My sinuses are now clear."

"I feel like I'm prepared to do an appendectomy," Amy said. "Or maybe brain surgery!"

Brad went over to the driver of the truck they would follow and handed him a list. He pointed across the large parking lot to the east, then toward East Capitol Street and west. While Brad was coordinating with the truck team, Paul got some duct tape and put a set of booties on the ends of his staff. He did the same for Amy.

"I get a feeling this will be a good idea," he said.

"Okay," Brad said when he got back. "Mount up, we're heading out."

Paul felt like he was in a diving suit or space suit, moving and climbing in and out of a car with all the paper-like barrier clothing on. When they were all in, Brad pulled out and followed the truck toward the stadium.

"We're going to collect the ones we found here, first," he said. "Then we'll head back toward the Capitol Building. We'll see how well this works with these first few."

The truck stopped near the survivor shuffling around on the far side of the large parking lot. The men got out, dropped the rear gate and steps, and stood by.

"We get on the other side of him," Brad said, "or her, and see if we can prod him or her toward the truck. Speak softly. I don't know if they can understand language at this point, but maybe we can cajole them. Paul, Amy, use your sticks to gently push and steer them."

Everyone nodded at Brad's instructions, then spread out opposite the truck. They spoke softly: "move to the truck," "let's go to the truck," and similar encouragements. Paul and Amy were in the center, where their staffs would be effective.

The survivor stopped shuffling and turned to look at Amy and Paul. Its jaw hung loosely and long hair hung in tangled strands across its face. It stopped, looked, then turned toward the truck.

Paul used his staff to nudge the survivor toward the truck. It took a step. The team repeated their soft encouragements. It turned its head and glanced back at Paul. Then it took a few more steps.

Fifteen minutes later, the survivor finally made it up the steps and into the back of the truck. Ten more minutes after that, they team managed to get the survivor to sit on the bench. It looked at Paul and Amy again as the steps were swung up and the gate closed.

"We're going to need more booties," Amy said, looking at the coverings on her shoes.

Paul lifted his left foot to see the underside of his bootie.

"Oh, gross!" he said. He walked back to where the survivor had been walking back and forth in an endless loop. The ground was covered in a black filth. He could smell the stench, even through the mentholated cream. And they had all just walked through that.

Paul took his booties off and removed the bootie from one end of his staff. It was now smeared with a black stain. He grabbed a plastic bag from the car, stuffed his soiled booties into it, and collected the booties from the rest of the team. Then he taped a fresh bootie to his staff.

Brad tied the bag of soiled items to the roof rack of his Chevy.

"I don't want these in the car," he said. "No amount of plastic will contain that smell."

They got back in the Chevy and followed the truck. The team collected three more survivors from the area around the stadium, being more careful to avoid getting the filth on their protective clothing.

When they got back to the high school to deliver their first batch, another team had set up a shelter. This team met them in full environment suits and helped get the survivors off the truck and through the shelter. When the survivors came out the other side, they were naked but covered with paper robes. Another team took the survivors into the showers, men on one side and women on the other.

Once the four survivors from Paul's team reached the showers, the team in the environment suits hosed down the inside of the shelter with chemical disinfectants and hauled away the remains of the clothing in airtight containers.

Paul pulled down his mask and sniffed. Most of the smell was gone, and it was tolerable to breath without the mask.

Brad had wrangled more booties and two more sticks, similar in length to Paul's and Amy's. They taped booties to the ends of those, too.

"Might as well get your lunch," Brad said. "This'll be slow going. We might get six more before the end of the day at this rate."

The truck team had hosed down and scrubbed out the back of the truck and was now eating lunch.

#

After eating, they all went into the high school to use the facilities. Paul stopped at one of the tables by the door on the way out to see how things worked inside.

The survivors had gone through the showers and were now dressed in loose sweatpants and sweatshirts, with slippers. Most were now sitting at one of the tables and helpers were trying to feed them what looked like baby food. *Probably a good idea,* Paul thought, *since they hadn't eaten in a long time.*

Once they took a bite of the food and swallowed it, they seemed interested in having more.

A female survivor stool alone. She'd been washed and given clean sweats to wear but hadn't yet made it to the lunch table. One of the workers, a woman Paul recognized from the church nursery, was speaking softly to the survivor and gesturing toward a table. The survivor continued to stand still, her lank hair covering her face. Casually, automatically, the worker reached out and brushed the survivor's hair back.

Then the worker fell to the floor, screaming.

Paul hurried over to help. A nurse, fully clothed in protective gear, got there at the same time.

"What's the matter with her?" Paul asked.

"She isn't wearing latex gloves," the nurse replied. "She touched the survivor with her bare hand."

The nurse did a quick examination of the woman.

"Can you help me get her to the clinic down the hall?" she asked Paul.

"You bet," he said and got hold of her under her shoulders. The nurse took her feet and they moved her out of the gym quickly.

In the clinic, Paul and the nurse put the woman—Maria, that was her name—on a cot. The nurse restrained Maria with straps, then gave her an injection.

After a few moments, Maria settled down.

"Thanks for the help," the nurse said. "I can't believe she was out there without gloves, at least."

"So it isn't just the filth we're worried about," Paul said.

"No," the nurse said. "I suspected the survivors would be more than they appeared. Think about it. They haven't had food or water for over nine months, and yet they're still walking around. Yeah, they're skin and bones, but they should be long dead. This isn't normal."

"You got that right," Paul said. "Something about that black fog. There must be something left behind in the survivors."

Maria turned her head and looked at Paul. Her eyes glazed over with a black film. She tried to mumble something, then passed out.

"That's not good," the nurse said.

As Paul walked back through the gym, James Carson was there reinforcing the part of the procedures and process that require everyone to wear latex gloves, or more, when working with the survivors.

"That was scary," Paul said when James was finished talking to the site crew.

"We have to be so careful," James said. "We have limited supplies, limited capability. We have to make the best use of what we have. I just hope we don't lose Maria."

"Is this what you did in the military?"

"No," James said. "I was an Army officer. I went in after college, went to OCS and Armor school. I had a platoon, then a company. On my second deployment to Iraq, I was a battalion S3—that's operations."

"Oh."

"I got some training and a great job in Chicago after the war working in systems and process management."

"Chicago. Really? Were you there in The Troubles?"

"Yes. I survived it, but lost my wife and two daughters there. They were believers, so I know they are with Jesus now."

"I'm so glad you found your way to us, James."

#

They did manage to gather six more survivors before they called it a day. They got them back to the high school and through the cleanup process, even helped the truck team get the truck cleaned up and ready for the next day.

At the hotel, they made a quick report, then learned their assignments were about to rotate. For the next two days, Paul and Amy would help with the laundry team at the hotel. After the last few days, the change came as a relief.

TEN

Laundry Duty

PAUL AND AMY each got a list and a laundry cart after breakfast. Their task was to go through the list of room numbers and gather up the laundry. Another team would follow shortly, following the same list, and bring fresh sheets and towels to those rooms.

They used the utility elevators. Amy got off on the next to top floor, and Paul rode all the way up. It was a simple job. Go to the room, pick up the bundle of laundry in front of the door, put it in the cart, mark off the room number, move to the next room. Paul was only half done when the laundry cart was overflowing, so he went back to the elevator. When it arrived, the boy bringing the fresh sheets and towels came out.

"Hey," he said.

"Hey," Paul said. "I only got about half of them. Will be back."

"No problem," the other boy said. "It takes a bit to drop these off."

Paul got in and went down. Amy got in on the next floor.

"Easy job, eh?" Paul said.

"Nice change from the last few days," she said. "No staff, no backpack, no survivors. Just push the cart and load it. Push the cart and load it."

Paul chuckled. "I never would have dreamed laundry could be so relaxing."

They spent the day collecting laundry, with a break for lunch. When they finished a little early, they took a walk in the park across the street.

"I'd like to hear the reports when the teams come in today," Amy said.

"Me, too. I hope they're boring."

"Yeah, nice and boring, just like our day. Push the cart and loaded it, only with survivors instead of dirty laundry."

"If we keep up this pace, we can have most of the city back in a couple months."

"Except for the huge sulfurous animal tracks melted into the asphalt." Amy frowned.

"Yeah, except for that. Speaking of which, have you noticed how the tracks all seem to come from and go back to an underground metro station?"

Amy looked blankly at Paul.

"You do know that Washington, D.C. has a subway system, right? Just north of where we first saw tracks is the Foggy Bottom metro station. Union Station is another end of the underground metro trains."

"I hadn't really thought about it," she said. "I always equate subways with New York City. So you're saying whatever is making those tracks…is be using the underground subway tunnels?"

"It sure looks that way."

Amy thought a moment. "If that's true, that would mean the creature can travel all around the city without being seen, pop up for a meal, then vanish underground again."

"Creature, or creatures," Paul said. "We don't know how many there are. The subway tunnels could be full of those things."

They got back to the hotel in time to hear the first reports from returning teams. The first few reports were mostly boring, just as Paul had wished, but then a team reported that a couple of the survivors recorded earlier by the recon teams were dead now. Only bones and shredded clothing remained. One was by Washington Circle Park and the other a couple of blocks from Union Station.

"I think something is coming from somewhere down in the tunnels," Paul said, standing up. "I suspect they use the subway tunnels to move around the city and come up for food in the night."

A murmur swept through the room.

"I don't know what they are or how many, but judging from the footprints, they must be huge," Paul continued. "If they can get anywhere in the city using the tunnels, our processing sites may be in danger."

"How many are there? Two?" someone in the group asked.

A man near the back of the room stood and started walking to the front.

"I may have some insight," he said as he approached Elder Franklin. "I'm Dr. Ben Samuels. I used to be a faculty member in the Philosophy Department at the University of North Carolina. I taught and researched religion and folklore and I think I know what is coming out of the tunnels."

Paul could see Dr. Samuels had everyone's attention. The room was quiet. Dr. Samuels was a tall, slim, dark-haired man with a thick mustache and a several-days-old beard. He wore wire-rimmed glasses and he took these off and cleaned them with a cloth as he prepared to speak further.

"I believe," he began as he returned his glasses to their place on his face, "these are what we call hellhounds."

A collective gasp filled the room.

"You see, the behavior is consistent with that described in a number of ancient texts I've researched. Hellhounds are controlled by and serve a specific demon. The demon possesses humans, and those possessed are used to feed the hounds. The purpose of the hounds is to hunt down people and drag them to hell. As you have seen here, the city and its environs have been pretty well cleaned out."

Samuels looked around the room, seemingly surprised that they were all paying attention to him.

"These survivors, as we call them, are possessed and are—for all intents and purposes—lost to Satan. They are now just objects to further his objectives, at least that would be the perspective of whoever is working here."

Paul was still standing, frozen to his spot by the professor's pronouncement.

"You mentioned a demon," Paul said. "The hounds are controlled by a demon?"

"Yes," Samuels said. "A demon usually controls a pack of hellhounds."

"A pack?" Amy stood up next to Paul.

"Uh, considering the number of possessed in the city, there is likely a large pack working here. And with a pack this large, we probably have a powerful demon."

A number of people started talking, a few were shouting. Elder Franklin stood and held up his hands.

"Please," he said. "Quiet, please."

When the uproar in the room subsided, the elder turned to the professor.

"Hellhounds and demons. Isn't this folklore? Are you certain?"

"For most people, including Christians, Satan was folklore until last year," Samuels said. "This folklore is staring us straight in the face now."

"How do we ..." the elder began. He stopped, cleared his throat, and tried again. "How do we kill the hellhounds?"

"With a consecrated weapon," Samuels said.

"A consecrated ...?" The elder let out a sigh. "Well. That puts a very different spin on things," Franklin said. "This will impact our plans and how we do our work."

Franklin called up the leadership of the mission, including Paul's parents and directed them to a smaller conference room.

"This meeting is over," Franklin said. "We will go over this information and will have updates to our plan by morning."

#

"Demons and hellhounds," Paul said as he and Amy left the room. "So much for our nice normal mission trip."

Amy shrugged. "We've faced stuff like that before. We can fight them and we can kill them. Or rather, *you* can kill them. You and the Holy Spirit through you."

Paul stopped in his tracks. "Me? How?"

Amy looked at him squarely. "Full of questions, aren't you? Paul, you're a smart boy, but you can be really dense sometimes. Didn't you hear what Dr. Samuels said? To kill a hellhound, you need a consecrated weapon—like your sword. It's an angel blade. And it came to you, not me or anyone else."

Paul swallowed hard. "What about the demon? How will we deal with it?"

"I don't know. I guess God will show us when the time comes.'

A demon and his hellhounds, prowling beneath the city in a network of underground tunnels, surfacing only to drag victims to hell. And against that, Paul and his sword.

"I have a feeling I'm not going to sleep well tonight," Paul said.

#

The next day, one of the teams did not make it back for the evening.

The team had been doing recon near the Dupont Circle area. Earlier in the day they'd checked in with the other school site. One of the other recon teams had seen them.

"They said they found a lot of survivors around Dupont Circle," said Dan, the leader of the other team. "They found piles of remains there, too."

Elder Franklin came in then. The missing team report brought him hustling in from elsewhere in the hotel.

"What are the chances of getting some teams out there before dark to see if we can find them?" he asked.

"Ours can head back out, after we gas up," Dan said.

Another team lead raised his hand. "We're all ready."

"Good. We have a couple of radios. Check with Randy, he can get you set up. We have a base station here and can track your progress. Get moving."

Paul and Amy followed Elder Franklin to the room where the radio was set up. The recon teams headed out and did radio checks on the way. After about a half hour, they checked in again. They were near Dupont Circle. One team was taking some side streets, circling the park. The other went directly to the circle and scouted around. They found the large number of survivors reported earlier, but little else.

The second team came around and scouted up to the metro station. They reported finding the car of the missing team.

"The doors are open. We're not approaching yet. Have Team Two come up here."

The operator at the base station relayed the information and the other team moved to link up.

"They're here," the first team called after a few minutes. "We're going to approach the vehicle now."

The room was silent for what seemed forever. Then a squawk came across and Team One reported in.

"No one at the vehicle. Blood everywhere. The doors to the car have been torn open. Scorch tracks all over the place, more than one set. We grabbed tablets and notebooks and we're getting out of here."

"Roger," the operator said.

"Tell them to get on the main roads and get back now," the elder said.

The operator relayed the orders.

Both teams gave a "Roger, Out." Then the radio was silent.

Elder Franklin turned from the radio and noticed Paul and Amy. They both had shocked looks on their faces.

"You shouldn't have been eavesdropping," he said, but he didn't sound angry. "Get yourselves to supper."

They obeyed, but didn't eat well. After the evening meal, Elder Franklin called everyone to gather in the large conference room.

"We lost a recon team today," he said. "We don't know their status and we don't know what happened. We hope their notes will help tell us what they found. For now, though, we're going to avoid the Dupont Circle area. And we're going to have our recon teams go out in pairs, from now on. The materiel we got from the office buildings by the Capitol included radios. We'll get the rest of them out, put fresh batteries in them, and get them to the recon teams.

"There is something out there and we need to be more careful and watch out for each other."

The elder raised his hand and bowed his head.

"Let us pray. Our Father in Heaven, please look after our lost people. If they have been taken, please accept them into Your bosom. Watch over our teams as we continue to try to do Your work and save these poor souls. Help us with strength and courage, Father, and give us the wisdom to better deal with our challenges these next few days.

"We also pray for healing for our sister, Maria, who was struck down by whatever force animates the survivors. We ask that You touch her with Your gentle spirit and ease her suffering.

"We ask these things in the name of Your Son, Jesus Christ. Amen."

The crowd in the room repeated, "Amen."

Paul was quiet on the stairs back to their floors.

"Are thoughts still a penny?" Amy asked when they stopped at her floor. She held up a little bit of copper.

"Oh, I'm not sure what to think, yet," Paul said. He took the penny and gazed at it, contemplating the old value and his thoughts. "We lost a team. Probably to those hellhounds. The adults are armed and will be nervous. But their guns won't help them if it's hellhounds they're dealing with."

"Your sword is the only thing I can think of that will kill them, according to the mythology. That's not to say I want you to go hunting them."

"I don't think there's any danger of that."

"So what do you have in mind?"

"I think we go back out tomorrow and collect some more survivors. We see what kind of progress they're making at the site. I'd like to get a look at the first ones we brought in."

"Sounds like a plan," she said. "See you tomorrow."

She ducked through the door. Paul paused before going up the next flight of stairs. *Was I hoping for another kiss on the cheek?* he asked himself.

#

They showed up in the parking lot after breakfast with new bags of protective clothing and fresh booties taped to the staffs, ready to gather some more survivors.

"So how was laundry duty?" Brad asked.

"Fine," Paul said. "It was a nice break. Still, it was hard to stay away from the reports at the end of the day."

"We were scrounging food and supplies from area markets," Janet said. "You won't believe the horrid smells coming from some parts of those grocery stores. Not as bad as survivors, but bad."

"We'll start at the high school this morning," Brad said. "Then we'll go toward the Capitol collecting. The team from the last couple of days got a lot of survivors."

Once they were all in, Brad took the quick route to the high school. The truck team wasn't ready yet, so Paul and Amy went inside to see how things were going.

Gary came up to them.

"You need to see that first guy you brought in," he said. "We have him talking a little. His name is Daryll." Gary pointed to a table across the gym. "He's there. Go see him."

A pastor was talking to Daryll, gently asking questions and engaging him.

Daryll turned and looked at Paul and Amy as they approached. He seemed to recognize them and grew more alert. Paul smiled at him and nodded.

"How are you, Daryll?" Paul asked.

Daryll's jaw moved up and down a few times. Then he seemed to struggle to say something. Finally, he spoke.

"He wants you," Daryll said. He pointed his hand at Paul and Amy.

The pastor, shocked, dropped his jaw. Then he composed himself. "Who wants them, Daryll?"

Daryll's breath trembled and he just said, "He!" Daryll then turned back to the pastor, his body seized up and he collapsed on the table.

ELEVEN

Progress

"I CAN'T EXPLAIN it," Gary said. "Daryll's been making great progress. He's been able to take care of his own sanitary needs, and shower and dress himself. We keep someone around to watch over him and the other men, but he needs little help now. That episode he just had—I haven't seen anything like it from any of the survivors."

Paul nodded. He and Amy had moved away from Daryll's table. Amy seemed shaken by Daryll's strange behavior and his collapse. Paul felt pretty shaken himself, but he kept his voice calm as he asked, "Are the survivors making good progress overall?"

"Some of them are. Others are slower. We know some of the first names. None of the last names yet."

"What kind of work are the pastors doing so far?" Paul asked.

"They're usually praying over them," Gary said. "They ask questions, try to get a response, get some interaction going. That seems to work. The more they get cleaned up, eat regularly, all that, the more alert and responsive they become. It's just slow."

"Must be frustrating," Amy said.

"Yes. But we pray a lot." Gary said. "That guy, James Carson, he's done a lot with helping. He works with the staff here to streamline and improve the process. Thanks to him, we're able to get survivors cleaned up, and transitioned into the facility more quickly. We haven't had any more incidents like with Maria. We may get to the point we don't have to worry about that anymore, but I think that's a way down the road."

Paul noticed that Daryll was rousing. He didn't try to approach again, but let the pastor continue his work with Daryll.

He and Amy left the gym and met with Brad.

"We're ready to go," Brad said. He held up his sheet. "Here's the list. Mount up."

They followed the truck down East Capitol Street to Lincoln Park, and they started gathering survivors. They got six in the truck and took those back to the high school, then ate lunch and cleaned out the truck. After lunch they went back to the east side of Lincoln Park. They had two more in the truck when they found an unrecorded survivor along the sidewalk at the intersection of East Capitol and Eighth Street.

"Strange," Brad said. "I thought we combed this area pretty thoroughly. How could we have missed one?"

Paul shook his head. "Yeah, that doesn't make sense. We would have seen that one easy all out in the open like that."

"Let's get him, anyway," Amy said.

Paul made notes on the location of this survivor, then got out with the rest of the team.

They used their usual tactic, getting on the opposite side from the truck and encouraging him to move toward the truck. This one moved better than most, with just a little prodding from Paul's staff.

Paul noticed that the ground beneath this survivor's pacing area was not as filthy as that of the other survivors he'd seen. There was an evident fifteen foot strip where the survivor moved back and forth, but it was hardly dirty at all.

Once the survivor was in the truck and the gate closed, Paul brought up his observation to Brad.

"I don't think we missed him at all," Paul said. "I think he moved here very recently. Look how clean the ground is in his area. And there's hardly any smell."

"Hmm. I wonder how he got here?"

The two of them went back to the survivor's spot and looked carefully at the ground surrounding it. They couldn't identify any obvious tracks or marks leading to the spot.

"We'll keep an eye on this one," Brad said. "I'll warn Gary when we get back. Let's get some more and wrap up for the day."

When they brought back a full load, Brad huddled with Gary as the survivors were unloaded from the truck. He pointed out the odd survivor to Gary and shared what they'd found and suspected.

"You'll want to keep a close eye on that one, Gary," Brad said. "With all the other odd things happening, we don't want any surprises."

"Got it, Brad. We'll watch him like a hawk."

#

At the hotel, Brad and his team shared what they'd discovered about the unrecorded survivor—his late arrival, the relative lack of filth and stench in his trail area, and now easy it had been to get him on the truck, almost as if he'd wanted to come.

"Have any other teams seen anything like this?" the elder asked.

All he got was shaking heads.

"Keep alert, then," Elder Franklin said. "Look out for unrecorded survivors. Make sure we watch them closely when we bring them in."

#

The next day, Brad's team got to the Capitol Building in their efforts to gather up survivors. They followed the truck to the west side of the building, where Paul had found a survivor in a ragged suit, the one Janet thought might be a congressman, going up and down steps.

The team got out of the car and climbed the stairs past the survivor, then moved to encourage him to go down to the truck.

"He's got a briefcase," Paul said through the heavily coated mask. "That might help identify him."

The survivor looked first at Paul, then at Amy, then turned to slowly move down the stairs. Paul gently prodded the survivor's back with his stick to keep him moving. "Come on, Congressman," he said.

The man stopped in his tracks, turned, and looked Paul right in the eye. His arms hung limply and his jaw was slack, but his gaze was sharp. A shiver ran down Paul's spine.

The team spoke softly to encourage him to turn and head to the truck, but he stayed put and continued staring at Paul.

Finally, after a couple of minutes, he turned and took a few more steps. He stopped, then stepped again. Once he almost missed a step, and it looked like he would topple over, but eventually the team guided him to the truck and onto a bench on the flatbed, and they got him to sit down.

The stairway survivor was the only one who gave them any trouble that morning. When the team returned with the morning survivors, Brad made sure Gary's crew was aware of the briefcase so they could try to get it and check the documents inside.

"That is going to be a nasty job," Gary said. "The case is about as bad as their clothing."

They ate their lunch and helped clean up the truck, the routine was almost automatic by now. Then they followed the truck back to the mall, working their way down toward the Washington Monument.

At the Hirshhorn Museum and Sculpture Garden, they found the survivor—evidently a woman—who kept trying to push through the main doors. The doors were marked "Pull." Paul shook his head as they maneuvered so they could herd the survivor toward the truck.

When the survivor turned from the building and walked away, the team started speaking soft encouragement and Paul readied his staff to gently push the survivor. At the far end of the survivor's path, it stopped, turned, and looked at Paul and Amy. The team continued speaking softly and tried to turn the survivor, but she just kept gazing at Paul and Amy.

Finally, though, the survivor turned and stepped out of its defined path and toward the truck. When the survivor was seated and the gate closed, the team headed back to the car.

Paul hadn't touched this survivor with his staff, so he didn't replace the bootie this time.

"Brad," he said as he climbed into the car, "this bit about the survivors looking at Amy and me is really getting annoying. Sometimes they look as if they're just about to say something."

"Far as I know, no one else is reporting that behavior," Brad said. "Something about you two gets their attention."

"We're famous with the survivors," Amy said. "Pretty soon, they'll be asking for our autographs."

They picked up a few more survivors and headed back to the high school. After unloading and cleaning up the truck, they went into the gym. Gary met them with a tablet in his hand.

"We got some documents out of the briefcase," he said. "They smelled awful, but we managed to get images with the tablet so we could look them over. Turns out that survivor was either a representative, or a representative's staff person. Once we get him talking, we should be able to sort that out."

"What did you do with the briefcase?" Paul asked.

"Disposed of it as we do the clothing and other stuff," Gary said. "We got images of all the documents, so nothing is lost. There's just no way we want to keep those papers. We get a residual scent in the gym as it is."

Paul couldn't tell if the gym had a scent. His nostrils and sinuses were overloaded with the mentholated cream smell.

"Any status on Daryll?"

"He's better," Gary said. "I bet in a couple more days, he'll be able to talk to you. He seems to have some kind of desire to see you and Amy again. The pastors are working on him to see if they can save him, get him to accept Christ. He keeps saying his sins are too great."

Gary waved around the room.

"There are a few others able to speak and the pastors are working with them, as well," he said.

Paul noticed that some of the survivors, some of the first ones recovered, were bringing plates of food to other survivors.

"You have survivors helping, now?"

"A little," Gary said. "Some are taking direction, so we have them serving meals. It gives them something to do. If we keep having this kind of progress, they will be doing a lot more to help out."

"How about the unrecorded survivor from yesterday?" Brad asked.

"He's just sitting, right now," Gary said, pointing at him a few tables away. "Like a lot of the new ones, he just sits. But he does look around a bit more than the others."

"The elder said we need to keep a close eye on him," Brad said. "No one else found any like him yet. But we may hear differently tonight."

Brad looked around, then at his team.

"We should head back to the hotel. Last call to use the facilities before we leave."

#

Another unrecorded survivor was found by one of the other teams and taken to the other site. That was the highlight of the evening reports. The warning to keep that survivor under close supervision was passed to the staff at the other site by the team bringing him in.

Some more survivor remains were found near Foggy Bottom and Union Station. Other than that, not much happened outside the routine, and no more teams went missing.

Elder Franklin was pleased and offered up a prayer of thanks. "We can only do what we feel is God's commission," he said. "I pray we can reclaim this city."

He also shared some good news. Maria, the woman who'd touched skin-to-skin with a survivor, was recovering. She couldn't remember what happened, but was getting care and prayers, with the hope of a full recovery.

TWELVE

Demon

PAUL AND AMY followed Elder Franklin out of the small conference room where teams made their reports.

"Sir," Paul said, "Amy and I would like to talk to you about these survivors and what we've seen."

"Certainly," he said. "Come into the office over here and we can talk."

"There are some things we need to share with you," Paul started, as they settled into chairs in the small office. "We told you before about all that we did during the Troubles."

The elder nodded and smiled. He had kind eyes and a ready smile. All Paul could hope, at this point, was that he had an open mind.

"The Adversary, Satan, made a total mess of things," Paul said. "Our community has only seen a very small part of that. We found zombies, some monk-like things, even aliens."

The elder nodded again. He'd heard the full story shortly after Paul and Amy had returned.

"What I'm thinking," Amy said, "is this demon may have been left behind and taken up residence in the underground tunnels, and now he's controlling the hellhounds from there."

"Hellhounds are a pretty serious matter," Elder Franklin said, his bushy white eyebrows crowding over his eyes.

"Paul can deal with the hellhounds," Amy blurted out.

The elder's bushy white eyebrows tried to climb over the top of his head.

"Really?"

"Sorry, Paul," Amy said.

Paul took a deep breath.

"It's okay, Amy," he said reaching into his pack. He pulled out the sword. The gleaming blade reflected the overhead lights across Elder Franklin's face. "We think this is an Angel Blade."

"May I?" the elder asked, holding out his hands. Paul carefully set the sword in his hands. "I've heard of these things in my life. Not many people talk about them, unless they are in some fantastic TV series or something. An Angel Blade! Did Gabriel give this to you?"

"How can you tell it is an Angel Blade?" Paul asked.

"I can feel the power," he said.

"Well, no, Gabriel didn't give it to us. Not directly, anyway. We picked it up in one of the twisted realities we went through. And this vest." Paul indicated the leather vest he wore. "I don't know if the vest is anything special. It's protected me from a lot of things."

Elder Franklin gently handed the sword back to Paul.

"Obviously, this is something you are meant to have and use," he said. "If my understanding of this is correct, the only thing that can kill a hellhound is an Angel Blade. If God placed this in your hands —no matter how that came about—He trusts you to use it for His purpose."

"We could use some guidance now," Paul said.

"Children," the elder said, "I'm an elder of the church for a good reason. I'm a man of God and I live by his word and try to pattern my life after Jesus Christ. I recognize the work of Satan. I pray several times a day for guidance and wisdom, especially in this place we are trying to save. Until now, I wasn't certain how we would stand against the evil that permeates this city." He scratched at his white head.

"But this puts a different spin on our efforts here. If the survivors are demon-possessed, and being used to feed the hellhounds, it changes how we must approach the salvation of these poor souls." He looked away for a moment. "That is, assuming we can save them.

It also means we have to change some of our practices to better protect our teams."

He slapped his hands on his knees and stood. "I'll consult with some of the pastors and others in the teams. Not everyone is prepared for the horror of what we face. We have a powerful weapon, but we need to develop a plan to put it to effective use."

Paul returned the sword to its place in it's sheath and stood. He felt like a huge weight had been lifted from his shoulders. It was a relief and a comfort.

"Thank you," he said to the elder. "Thank you so much for understanding."

"No problem, Paul, Amy. Let me think on this for a while. For now, you shouldn't miss your dinner. I'll let you know when I have some idea how to proceed."

#

"That went better than I expected," Paul said to Amy over dinner. "I expected to lose the sword to the adults."

"I think the elder is a great blessing to us," Amy said. "I hope he comes up with some good ideas soon. I thought I had ruined everything when I said you could deal with the," she lowered to a whisper, "dogs."

"No," Paul said. "It had to be done. I'm just floored he listened, heard, and understood."

Amy put her hand on his across the table.

"No matter what, Paul," she said, "I'll be right beside you."

Paul knew he was blushing. He glanced up at Amy and saw her smiling.

"Thanks," he managed to say.

#

The next two days were uneventful, other than more remains being found at recorded survivor locations. The high school sites were getting crowded, and most of the survivors gathered first were taking more of the work of caring for the later survivors. Some had finally accepted Jesus Christ and became much more alive and vibrant.

Those who hadn't come to Christ yet, still caused problems at times, according to Gary, like throwing food, shrieking, and knocking over tables. Those who did come to Christ were at peace and improving.

Daryll, though, was still reticent. The pastors worked on him and tried to get him to accept Christ. He could see the change in the other survivors, but just couldn't get past his own sinfulness.

At the end of the second day Paul came over and sat in front of Daryll.

"My name is Paul," he said. "My team brought you in that first day."

"I know. We all know about you and Amy."

"We who?" Paul asked.

"All of us."

"What do you know about us?"

"That he wants you."

"Who is this 'he'?"

"He who is our master."

Paul smiled at Daryll. "I hear you are having trouble accepting Christ."

"My sins are too great," Daryll said. "Christ could not accept me."

"That's not true," Paul said. "No sin is too great for God to forgive. All you have to do is believe in Christ. He died for you. He can save you."

"My sins are too great."

"What did you do before the Troubles?" Paul asked.

"I was a coach," he said. "That's where my sins are. I…used the boys I coached. I betrayed them. I couldn't help myself. My appetites were horrible and I couldn't resist them."

Paul's stomach churned, his jaw clenched, and he resisted the urge to turn away. *God, give me strength*, he pleaded. He took a deep, cleansing breath and looked at Daryll.

"But God forgives you, if you accept that," Paul said. "You just put those sins behind you. Accept his forgiveness and become a new person."

For a long time Daryll didn't speak. Paul waited and watched. Then, before his eyes, Daryll began to weep.

"All those boys," Daryll said, "Satan took them in the fog. He tortured them horribly and then took them. He left me here, burning inside. It was all my fault. How can God forgive me?"

Paul swallowed hard. "Because He is God. He has infinite love for us. He knows we are weak and He knows we need to lean on his strength. All you have to do is ask for His forgiveness and strength to go forward."

"But all those boys," Daryll sobbed.

"Some of them are lost," Paul said struggling to control his voice. He felt like falling to the floor and weeping right then. "Yes, that cannot be undone. But God offers His hand in forgiveness now. While you have a chance to live, to come to God, embrace Jesus, fill yourself with the Spirit, you can take it. Christ awaits and turns away no one."

"But, how?"

"Just ask, Daryll. Just ask." Paul felt he was pleading now. *Please, God. Help me.*

"What do I say?"

"Say this," Paul said. "Father God, forgive me of my sins."

Daryll repeated Paul's words, choking through his sobs.

"Father God, I know Your Son was given in sacrifice for my sins and I accept Jesus Christ into my heart as my savior and king."

Daryll, still racked with sobs, again repeated the words.

"Father God, my Lord Jesus, from now on, I will follow you and accept your sacrifice for my sins. I promise to live my life in worship to you."

As Daryll repeated the words, the earnestness of his heart shone on his face and a darkness left him. Tears still streamed down his cheeks, but his eyes were clear.

He knelt next to the table and rested his head on it.

"I feel a weight lifted from me," he said. "I no longer feel the bindings that have been on me so long."

"That's good, Daryll. That's good."

The pastor that had been working with Daryll came over. He put one hand on Paul's shoulder and the other on Daryll's.

"I didn't want to interrupt," he said. "I prayed for both of you. Welcome to the kingdom, Daryll."

Daryl looked up and smiled. Then his smile faded and he turned to Paul with an intense look.

"There are things you need to know, Paul," he said.

The words gave Paul a chill of dread. "About the hellhounds."

"Yes, and other things."

Suddenly Daryll slumpted to the floor, breathing heavily. "But, I'm exhausted."

"I'll be back," Paul said. He waved to a nurse to help Daryll. "We can talk more when you feel stronger."

#

"That was an incredible thing to watch," Amy said as they rode back to the hotel in Brad's car. "You could almost see the darkness leave him when he accepted Christ."

"I've never been involved in a conversion that powerful before," Paul said.

"I think we need to tell Elder Franklin. Maybe get him to come out with us to talk to Daryll."

"That might be good. He may want to hear what Daryll wants to share about the 'things' we need to know."

THIRTEEN

Rebuke

BY THE END of the next day Brad's team had collected almost all the survivors from around the reflecting pond. They encountered no problems and no human remains.

At the high school site, Paul and Amy helped clean the truck and then went into the gym. Elder Franklin walked in just then as well.

"I'm here to talk to your survivor," he said.

"That's great!" Paul said. He and Amy led him to the table where Daryll was talking to a pastor.

Daryll stood and greeted them.

"I'm so glad you came back," Daryll said. "There's so much you need to know."

"We brought Elder Franklin with us," Amy said. She provided the introductions. "Elder Franklin should hear what you have to say."

"Good," Daryll said. He waved at nearby chairs. "Please, have a seat."

"Paul told me of your salvation yesterday," the elder began. "We are all so pleased."

"Elder, Paul helped me loose binds to a horrible power that had hold of me for a long time." Daryll looked at his feet for a moment, then continued. "He also mentioned the hounds. Yes, there are hellhounds, and they are being controlled by one of the fallen. Somehow, after the Troubles, this one remained behind."

"Is he the only one?" asked the elder. "Or are there others?"

"I don't know. There might be others somewhere in the world. But he's the only one around here."

The elder sighed. "This is troubling news. I'm not sure what we can do against one of the fallen. We believe the hellhounds can be killed, but the fallen are immortal. I think the best we could hope for is to drive it out."

"Everyone you bring in—" Daryll gestured around the room at the other survivors sitting at tables—"all these blank-eyed people, they're still bound to this demon, just as I was. Even now, I can sense he tries to hold me again, to fill my mind with doubt and darkness. I cling to Jesus, my Lord and Savior, and he cannot get a grip. But these others don't have that. They're as much in his power as they ever were. I think you need to cast off the bindings. The fewer people he holds, the less power he has here."

"We have been trying," the elder said. "Our pastors are working with the survivors, giving them the path to salvation. Praying over them."

"The pastors are overwhelmed," Daryll said. "The moment they go to work on one person, another person goes into a shrieking fit, or knocks over tables and chairs. Then, when everyone is cleaning up the mess and settling the others down, the demon regains his hold on the survivors. The cycle starts all over again. And every day you crews bring even more survivors into the facility."

Franklin nodded. Paul looked around at the workers. He saw the weariness in their faces.

"You're right," the elder said after a long silence.

Franklin stood and clapped his hands loudly over his head to get everyone's attention.

"Let's try something," he said and waved over the other pastors. "Bring all the faithful we can spare over here. Let's try some prayer."

One of the workers started to protest, pointing to a survivor woman under a table smearing food on the floor. Franklin just shook his head and waved the worker over.

The people circled Daryll. Each person put a hand on the elder and held a hand out toward Daryll. The elder lead the prayer.

"Father," he began, holding his hand above Daryll's head, "our brother senses the presence of one of the fallen and we ask your help.

Cast this demon out of our presence. Keep him away from our flock. We rebuke him in the name of Your Son, Jesus Christ! Begone!"

An almost palpable shiver ran through the building. Some of the more recent survivors turned and looked toward the group praying over Daryll. Others sat in wonder. The woman smearing food on the floor stopped and sat back.

Daryll looked up.

"He's still out there, but not close." He looked around the room. "Your prayer had an impact."

Every survivor in the room was turned in their direction, some more alert and responsive than others.

A pastor waved the elder over to another survivor.

"Let's try it again with this lady," he said.

They gathered around her and the elder repeated the prayer and rebuke. Again, the effect was palpable. The very air shimmered in the gym.

The woman blinked and looked around, then she slumped to the floor.

"She needs food and rest," the pastor said, helping a nurse gather her up, "but she'll be just fine."

The group started moving through the gym praying and rebuking over survivors as directed by the pastor. While the direct impact on each survivor they prayed over was immediate and immense, the other survivors in the room were affected as well.

"The fallen is losing his grip here," the elder said. After ten prayers and rebukes, his hair was standing up as if from static and his piercing blue eyes crackled with energy. "I can't keep this up, though. We need to get back to the hotel and share this information with the others."

"Well, there is a little more you need to know," Daryll said. "This demon wants Paul and Amy. I don't know his plans, but his goal is to have them, and he means to achieve that goal. The hellhounds may play a role. Hiding Paul and Amy won't protect them."

"Do you know where he is?" the elder asked.

"Somewhere underground," Daryll said.

"Do you know his name?"

"No, I don't," Daryll said. "I'm sorry, I can't tell you more."

"You've done well, Daryll," the elder said. "Pray and recover. We appreciate you."

Elder Franklin, not thinking about it, reached out his hands and grabbed Daryll's hands and held them for a moment. He wasn't wearing gloves.

Paul and Amy gasped and tried to stop him, but it was too quick and they were too late.

Nothing happened.

They froze in place, looking at the elder's hands. Then they looked up at each other and smiles slowly took over their faces.

"Daryll," Paul said, "you're cured!"

The elder let out a booming laugh.

"I didn't even think about it," he said when he caught his breath. "Yes, Daryll, you must be cured. Whatever poison was in you from that fallen angel is gone now. Now let's get back to the hotel and share this good news."

#

"We're going to shift our efforts," the elder said to the crowd gathered in the large conference room. "For now, we'll pull our recon teams back. We have enough recorded survivors to keep us busy for a while, and we're going to slow down the gathering a little. What I believe we should do now is set up prayer squads. We need to work our way through the survivors we've gathered and cast off the bonds a fallen angel has placed on them."

A gasp went through the crowd. While many may have suspected demons may be involved, few had actually spoken of it. Elder Franklin had just broken the taboo and put the issue on the table.

"A prayer squad will move through the survivors praying and rebuking the demon holding on to the survivor," he said. "This will help speed the process of getting these poor souls back to normal and accepting Christ. The site pastors will direct the squads through the survivors and work from the earliest to the more recent. But we must, we must work to get these people to accept Christ. We are casting out the demon, but cannot leave an empty house. We must fill that house with Jesus or that demon will come back with a vengeance."

He raised his hands in praise.

"Believe me, this works! God's hand is in it and His power is great!" The elder's voice boomed and his face beamed. "You should have seen the impact God had at Eastern High School! Not only will this speed the process of saving these poor souls, but it'll weaken the demon we'll have to face later."

Whispers raced through the crowd. A man stood.

"Elder," he said, "are we to face a demon?"

"Yes," Elder Franklin said. "I suspect we can cast him back to the Adversary's domain, wherever that is. We need to know his name and call him by name to cast him out. First, though, we need to weaken him and strengthen our position. We do that by breaking his bonds on as many survivors as we can save."

A woman stood. "Is it that simple?" she asked.

"No. But for the part most of us will play, that is as much as we can do, and the best we can do. Others will have to face very specific dangers and will need our faith and prayers."

"How do our prayers help?" another woman asked.

"Have faith and call upon the Lord Jesus Christ. In His name, you can do anything," the elder said.

He looked over the mission team before him.

"I know we are getting tired and the work is very hard. We don't know what happened to the missing recon team," Franklin said. He looked at James Carson sitting at a nearby table. "James, here, has done a terrific job organizing the work in a way that keeps us safe and efficient, and we've done our best to rotate duties and give people a chance to rest. Unfortunately we are facing more than we anticipated."

A woman stood as if to speak. Tears filled her eyes and she sat back down. Paul recognized her. She was the mother of a missing recon team member. Elder Franklin smiled kindly at her.

"Let's have a good prayer and get some sleep tonight," he said. "We'll all feel better in the morning."

He raised his hands. "Father, we come before You struggling for hope and fading in our faith. It has been a hard mission so far. But today, You delivered into our hands a saved survivor. A man who accepted Christ and who gave us insight into what we face. And You have provided Your soldiers who carry Your banner into this battle.

"We need Your help, Father. We need Your infinite love and presence in our lives and in our hearts. Please grant us the strength and wisdom only You can give. Show us Your plan and Your purpose. We humble ourselves before You and ask for this in Your Son's holy name, Jesus Christ. Amen."

The crowd chorused, "Amen."

#

The prayer squads made tremendous progress in the three sites, getting survivors cleared and "touchable." Survivors who were completely healed recovered more quickly and were able to turn to help other survivors. Some even joined prayer squads.

Paul and Amy observed the activity at the high school after another day of gathering survivors. They were the only team bringing in survivors at this site, since the other participants had been re-assigned to prayer squads. The squads slowly worked through the populations of the site, each handling only about five or six survivors a day. Prayer and rebuke cost the squads in strength and stamina. The squad members were hauled back to the hotel at the end of the day, exhausted.

Paul noticed the workers smiling more at the site, though, since there were fewer incidents with the survivors shrieking or throwing food.

Amy pointed at a man sitting at one of the tables. "Isn't that the unrecorded one we picked up a few days ago?"

"Yeah," Paul said. The man was looking around the room, watching the activity, while everyone else around him was engaged in something. Paul thought he acted completely detached and looked smug and contemptuous of his surroundings.

Paul found one of the pastors and asked about the man.

"We've been working on him," the pastor said. "We prayed and rebuked and prayed some more, then we talked to him about salvation and accepting Christ. No luck, so far. No one is trying to touch him, though. He just doesn't seem, uh, clear or clean. He doesn't throw fits like some of the others have done, but I'm pretty sure the demon still has a hold on him."

Paul nodded. "Yeah, I can see why. Did he give you a name?"

"He said his name is William Bolt."

Paul and Amy went over to him.

"Hello, William," Paul said. "I'm …"

"Paul," William said. "And she is Amy. I know."

Something felt unsettling to Paul. William was far more clear-headed than any of the other survivors they had brought in, but he was off-putting in voice and manner, and his face was hard.

"I see," Paul said. "May we ask you a few questions?"

The man smiled, a cold, confident smile that chilled Paul's blood. "You can ask me whatever you like."

"How do you know who we are? Did someone here tell you?"

"No, I know who you are because *he* told me," William said.

"He?" Paul said. "He, who?"

"The magnificent ruler of this place, his highness."

"Do you know his name?"

"Yes."

Paul waited. William just looked at him, then gave another contemptuous smile. "Do you actually expect me to give it to you? Really, Paul, you are such a child."

Paul felt like a child. He felt small and weak and hopelessly outclassed.

"Do you—do you remember when we found you and brought you here a few days ago?" Amy asked. Her voice sounded uncertain and Paul suspected she'd spoken just to change the subject.

"Of course," William said. "I was deliberately taken to a location where you would find me and bring me in."

Paul suspected as much, but hearing the words made him uneasy. The demon *wanted* William to be here. It was all part of his plan.

"Yes, Paul. It is his plan. You should have stayed in your little community with your gardens, your solar power, and your church and friends. This mission was just a supreme waste of lives, fuel, and time. You have no hope of clearing this city. It belongs to my master and will stay that way."

William grinned and his eyes darkened.

"But because you did come, he can take you—just like that recon team you lost. My master will delight in your torture before he delivers you to Satan. Satan will reward my master for bringing you to him, and my master will reward me for helping. All your effort, all your work and pain, will go for naught because your destiny is to die at my master's hands."

"Tell us the name of your 'ruler,'" Paul said with more force than he felt.

"No," William spat. "What kind of fool do you think I am? Child. My work here is done. I have the information my master needs. I know the hotel you use, I know where your sites are, I know the names of the workers." He raised his voice. "My master will now come for you all."

William stood and started moving toward the entrance. Paul and Amy slowly gave ground. James Carson appeared at Paul's side and inserted himself between Paul and William.

"Stop right there," Carson said. He held up his prosthetic arm. He wore latex gloves, even on that hand. William pushed forward into Carson's hand. Carson stood firm.

"Oh, yes, the 'wounded warrior.' The efficiency expert." William said. His lips twisted into a sneer. "How pathetic."

William brought his hand up to touch Carson's face, but Amy quickly caught the arm with her staff and pushed it away.

"Out of my way you pathetic, weak, ignorant fools!"

Paul was at a loss. What more could he do? He could see the workers and survivors in the gym all standing, watching this exchange.

Then he noticed a vibration from his pack. His first thought was it felt like a cell phone set on vibrate. But of course it had been a year or more since he's seen a functioning cell phone.

He reached over his shoulder and his hand touched the hilt of his sword. It was vibrating. He grasped the hilt and pulled the sword from the sheath. It glowed, as it once had. A bright blue light shone from it. He gently pushed past Carson and held the blade point up between himself and William. Blue flames started licked along the blade.

"Father, God," Paul began. He could feel the Holy Spirit fill him. He stared intently into the eyes of William. William's haughty look began to falter. "Please, be with me. Help me confront this presence."

Paul took a deep breath. The blue glow from the sword increased to a blinding intensity. Blue flames licked up the blade and shot into the air above.

"Demon! Leave this man! I rebuke you and command, in the Holy Name of Jesus Christ, Son of the Living God, begone!"

FOURTEEN

God's Soldiers

WILLIAM FLUNG out his arms and wrenched his head back as a bright beam of blue energy flowed from the sword to the middle of his chest. Rays of blue light shot from his eyes and mouth and finger tips. Smoke curled above his body.

The intense blue light from the sword went out, as though someone threw a switch. For a moment is seemed that the world had gone black, but that was only because the sword's light had dazzled Paul's eyes. The gym was now awash in normal light, which seemed entirely too dark.

William dropped to the floor and lay still.

Oh, God, Paul thought, *I didn't kill him, did I?*

A nurse and helpers nearby immediately came to William's aid. The nurse checked his breathing and pulse, then directed a helper to start chest compressions as she placed a plastic mask over William's mouth and nose and started squeezing a large rubber bulb.

Paul tucked the sword back into its sheath and watched as they worked on William on the floor.

"That was impressive," Amy said close to Paul's ear. "And I've seen it work before!"

After a few minutes, William eyes fluttered open and he looked up at Paul. He worked his jaw, trying to speak. Paul hoped against hope that William would be glad to be free. Finally, he muttered something.

"I'm empty!" he said, glaring hate at Paul. Then he passed out.

"We'll take him to the clinic for the evening," the nurse said, trying to avoid looking directly at Paul. "We can monitor him through the night there. He should be all right, but it may take a few days."

"I have no doubt he will be fine," Paul said. "He's just in shock. We ripped out the evil hold over him the hard way."

Paul stood and turned to leave. Everyone in the room who had their wits about them stared at Paul. Some applauded. Others looked concerned. Paul felt his face blushing.

"How did you do that?" someone demanded. "Where did that sword come from?"

Paul heard some angry murmurs from a small group of people across the gym.

"Uh-oh," Amy said. She put her arm in his and helped him start moving toward the exit. Paul just nodded and waved and they escaped out the door.

"What was that?" Brad asked at the car. "Was there a power surge in the gym?"

"It's a little something we picked up during the Troubles," Paul said ducking into the car. "Works well."

Paul kept his head down, but he could feel Brad's stare. His cheeks burned. Amy held his hand and sat close, shielding, protective.

"God's soldiers," Brad said. "Not what you would expect."

When they returned to the hotel, Paul and Amy shared their experience with William during the evening meeting. Amy said she knew there were at least two more unrecorded survivors found elsewhere.

"Maybe Paul and I need to go to each of the other sites and see if this will work on those survivors, too?"

"That's a thought," Elder Franklin said. "I'd like to see if we can get more information from William first. Could you check on William tomorrow and see if he's more forthcoming?"

"Sure," Paul said. "I'm hoping that the rebuke we did will shake off the demon's hold enough that William will tell us its name."

"That would be very useful. If we have its name, we can do more damage to it. With God's help, the name will give us the ability to send it back to wherever it belongs. Wherever God wants it."

On the way to dinner, Paul felt shaky and weak. Amy kept an arm around his as they walked.

"I feel like we made a turn," Paul told Amy as they quickly ate. "Like we exposed one of the demon's secret weapons and weakened him."

"So, what's next?" Amy asked.

"We're going hunting," Paul said. "We need to find out what we can do against the hellhounds, where they come from, and we need to draw the demon's attention from the rest of the mission."

"Hunting, eh?" Amy looked at him. "You told me the other day that you wouldn't do that."

"Things change."

"When do we go?"

"Tomorrow. First, we need to see if we can get William to give up the demon's name. Then we'll head out from Eastern High School."

He took a deep breath. He felt steadier after eating, more in control.

"Pack up some clothing and food," Paul said. "We'll ride out with Brad and Janet in the morning, just won't go out to gather survivors."

#

After dinner, Paul packed his backpack while the rest of the family watched an old DVD movie on the TV in the main room of their suite. He tightly rolled a couple changes of clothes into the bottom, then packed in the rest of the things he thought he should carry, including his light sleeping bag.

He checked the leather vest he wore almost constantly. There were some sweat stains, and a number of scars from previous battles, but it still fit. He couldn't imagine going without it. It provided a security he knew he needed in the field.

The Old Timer was still in his pocket, and he checked the sword in its sheath in the backpack. Last, he tucked a light jacket into the top of the pack, just in case of rain or bad weather, and the pair of binoculars.

He set the pack next to his bed. Mom stood in the door looking at him. She came and sat on the bed, indicating Paul should sit, too.

"You and Amy are not planning to come back from the city tomorrow," she said. Paul could see her eyes were red-rimmed. She'd been crying.

"No, Mom," he said. "We have to find out more. We may have to fight."

"I know," she said. "I'm your mother, I know these things. I figured out what was going on when Elder Franklin said God sent his soldiers. I knew he meant you."

She put an arm gently around her firstborn.

"I knew you and Amy—and Joe—were involved in something very important during the Troubles." She wiped tears with a tissue she had in her other hand. "God chose you. He will be with you. My best hope is that you keep your faith, do what God tasks you to do, and come home when the work is done."

"I will, Mom," Paul said. "The Lord God will provide. That was something we depended on in the Troubles, and God did provide. We may not have angelic help, but we have God's love and some tools."

He pulled out the Old Timer and showed it to her.

"A man we met in the Troubles gave this to me. His grandfather gave it to him. It was precious to him. The man gave it to me because he knew I needed it, and he had faith it would help us."

He put the knife back in his pocket, then pointed at the staff.

"Just like the staff, and this vest. The'are things we found or bought or someone gave us to help us survive and accomplish God's mission for us. God will provide."

"I have no doubt you will do what God needs you to do, Paul," she said. "But I need you to promise me something."

"Okay."

"I want you to promise me that you will take care of Amy and bring her home with you. I don't think she should go with you, but I know she will."

"I promise, Mom," Paul said. "But I can only do what God wills. And, to be honest, I couldn't go do what I need to do without her at my side."

"I have a feeling that will be the case for a very long time," Mom said. She leaned toward him and kissed his head. "I love you, son."

She got up and left the room.

What did she mean by that?

#

Gary was waiting outside the gym when they arrived in the morning and directed Paul and Amy to the clinic.

"William is still up there, but recovering well," he said.

When they arrived at the clinic, William was propped up in a sitting position on a bed. He looked tired, but was interacting with the caregiver in the room.

"May we come in?" Paul asked.

William looked at them in the door, then nodded.

"I'm not really glad to see you," he said. "You ripped out something and it hurt. I'll be okay, though. That's what they tell me."

"This demon, the one you called your master here, had a very tight hold on you," Paul said. "We need to know the name of this demon."

"I guessed you would be back to ask that."

"So, do you remember the name?" Amy asked.

"Yes," William said. "Do you really understand what you ask? That name, that is just the beginning."

"Yes," Paul said, "we're prepared."

"I very much doubt it. He rules here. He has hellhounds, and imps, and he plans to use those hounds to drag you two to hell."

"Kicking and screaming, I'm sure," Paul said, smiling at Amy.

"Don't get cute, Paul," William pointed his finger at Paul's chest. "This is serious. Once you and Amy are in hell, my master will possess more and expand his rule on Earth. He plans to earn great favor from Satan for taking you two."

"Taking it seriously," Paul said. "Why were you moved to where we picked you up? Did you master want you in our site?"

"He used me as a spy," William said. "He watched what you and your teams were doing. Your work angers him. He is losing his possessions. He will want them back. There are others like me, who are spying in your other areas."

"Do you know where your master is? Where does he stay?" Amy asked.

"Underneath, in the tunnels," William said. "He doesn't worry. You'll never survive trying to go down to get him. The hellhounds will probably take you. If they don't, there are others who stay close and protect him."

"We won't worry about that," Paul said. "We have God on our side and we will follow where he leads."

"You're a fool, then," William said. "The only thing you can count on is yourself. No god will save you or protect you from my master, or the others like him. You know, don't you, there are more like my master on Earth? Satan left a lot of his followers behind. You all will be their slaves."

"We cleared your master's hold on you, didn't we?" Paul said. "We can help you, get you into a relationship with God. We can help you get better."

"You cannot help me," William said. "I need no help."

"What did you do before the Troubles, William?" Amy asked.

"I was a United States Senator. I held power. I was rich. I had three houses. I took huge payments from supporters and voted for bills and resolutions that benefited them. I was proud of what I had and what I did. I lied to my constituents and was re-elected several times, and they were fools because their support just made me richer."

"Do you regret any of that?" Paul asked. "Do you want to confess that to Christ and ask his forgiveness?"

"Are you kidding?" William said. "When I go back to my master, I will be powerful again. I will lead legions of demons and imps and do his bidding. Why would I want to give that up?"

"We thought we could help you come back to God, receive forgiveness and His love," Amy said. "Don't you want that?"

"I want nothing from you. As soon as I'm able, I will go back to my master. Leave now."

"I still need the name of that demon," Paul said.

"You won't get it from me."

"I think I can persuade you," Paul said. He reached over his shoulder and drew the sword. It glowed blue.

Williams eyes widened and he cringed back in the bed.

"Your master has been regaining some hold on you, hasn't he?"

"Go away! Leave now!"

"I need the name of your master." The sword's glow intensified and flames began to lick along the blade. "Do we need to clean you out again?"

"No!"

Flames leaped from the sword and touched William on the head and chest.

"Give me the name," Paul said. "Now."

"No," William said, but with less confidence.

"Now," Paul repeated.

"Nelchael," William whispered as he writhed in agony from the flames from the sword.

"Thank you," Paul said. He returned the sword to the sheath.

"William, you should seriously consider giving yourself over to Jesus Christ now," Amy said. "He, at least, is forgiving and loving. I doubt Nelchael will be."

Back in the gym, Paul found Gary.

"William is a hard case," Paul said. "He plans to run back to the demon as soon as he's able."

Paul and Amy shared what they learned from William.

"We just got a message on the radios from the hotel," Gary said. "That professor from UNC said we should gather all the salt we can find and salt the perimeter of the facilities. It is supposed to keep the hellhounds and others out."

"That would take a lot of salt," Amy said.

"Yeah," Gary said. "I have a couple teams out now looking for salt. The other sites are getting salt, too."

"I hope that helps," Paul said, just as Brad came up.

"Hope what helps?" he asked.

"We're going to salt the perimeter of the facility," Gary said. He explained the radio message again.

"Can't hurt, I guess. Should keep hellhounds away," Brad said.

"Might keep William here, too," Paul said. "Look, we got the name of the demon, assuming William didn't lie to us. Nelcheal." Paul grabbed a piece of paper and a pen from a nearby table and wrote the name on it. "Brad, can you get that information to Elder Franklin and Dr. Samuels?"

"Sure," Brad said and took the paper.

"Put salt across the bridges, too," Paul said. "Don't let the hellhounds cross the bridges."

"Good idea," Brad said. "Aren't you coming back with us tonight?"

"No," Paul said. "There's something we have to do."

FIFTEEN

Hunting

PAUL SET HIS PACK on his back and checked the straps. He reached up with his right hand and found the hilt of the sword. Then he clipped a face mask onto a loop on one of his straps.

"Might be a good idea to keep the truck teams and gatherers near the site for the next few days," he told Gary. "Oh, yeah, and check your salt before sunset each night. Make sure the lines are intact."

Gary looked troubled. "Are you two sure about this?"

"We're sure," said Paul. "We've done this sort of thing before, during the Troubles. We have to find out if we can fight these hellhounds, and try to take the demon's attention off the recovery sites. God will protect us and provide for us. He always has."

"All right," Gary said. "Have fun hunting hellhounds. Good luck, and God speed! "

"Thanks," said Amy. "And thanks for the food. We'll be back in a couple of days, God willing. Pray for us."

"That's a given," said Gary.

#

After leaving the gym, Paul and Amy followed the road north, walking on the east side of the football stadium, across Constitution Avenue, and through a parking lot-cum-basketball courts next to another classroom building. Then they turned west on C Street.

"We'll start at Union Station," Paul said. "There were a lot of survivors there, so I bet we'll get a hellhound tonight."

"I'd be lying if I said I looked forward to it," Amy said. "But I agree, we'll mostly likely find one. Or one will find us."

They continued west. Along the way, they found a place where a survivor had beoame a meal for a hound.

"I thought this street was cleared," Paul said. "And this is pretty close to the recovery site." He pointed to scorched tracks coming to the remains and heading back toward Union Station.

"Bet the demon moved some survivors into cleared areas," Amy said. "Just to keep the hounds in food. Notice the smear of filth that shows where the survivor had been pacing. Not as much as usual. The survivor wasn't here for long."

They followed the hellhound trail, passing neighborhoods of row houses and continuing west. At Eighth Street, the trail crossed the parking lot of the Capitol Hill Hospital, wandered among the abandoned vehicles, then continued on the south sidewalk on C Street.

At Stanton Park, the trail went straight into the dry grass, leaving large, scorched areas around the tracks. It turned northwest, then, down Massachusetts Avenue. They could see Union Station.

"Let's try to keep out of sight," Paul said, "in case the demon has any spies hanging out there."

An apartment building to their right had a brick circular driveway. It was next to a gas station on the corner of Second Street. They entered the apartment building, climbed up the front stairs, and found an apartment on the top floor on the northwest side of the building. Paul led the way through the apartment to a room looking out toward the station. A window gave a good view of the front of Union Station. Paul pulled out his binoculars.

He scanned across the front of the station and Columbus Circle. There was a survivor there, near the far end of the circle. The trail they had followed from C Street was visible with the binoculars. It led into the front of the station. But it wasn't the only trail. The entry of the station was covered with hellhound tracks going in and out.

He handed the binoculars to Amy.

"There's a survivor," he said, "on the other end of Columbus Circle. But can you see all the tracks in front of the station entrance? The trails go off in all directions."

"Yeah," she said, still scanning.

"I wonder how many hounds are around here?"

Amy thought for a moment. "Could two make all that? Three?"

"I don't know. But this would be a good place to hold up and watch for the hounds. Salt the entries and the window sills and we could be pretty safe, I think."

"Did you bring salt?"

"No. Did you?"

"No."

Paul looked outside for a moment. "It's still early in the day. We can probably find enough nearby. What do you think?"

"The most likely places around here are all the little cafes and restaurants. I noticed quite a few a block or so back down the avenue."

"Can you think of anything else we should hunt down?"

"If we're going to be here tonight, we should get bottles of water. Might be some in the gas station."

"We should probably clean this room up a bit, too. Everything we touch here is covered in dust. Let's see what we can find in these apartments."

They found a couple of vacuums and some cleaning products. There was still power to the building, so they used the vacuums to clear out as much of the accumulated dust in the chosen room as possible. While Amy went to the apartment's bathroom to clean, Paul wiped down all the surfaces they would use in the room. Then the two of them worked together to move most of the furniture to other rooms and bring a couple of mattresses from other apartments.

"That should work," Amy said, wiping sweat from her brow with the back of her hand. She spread her sleeping bag out on one of the mattresses. "I get this one."

Paul laughed and pulled his bag out and spread it out on the other mattress. He returned to the window with his binoculars. The survivor on the far end of Columbus Circle was still there. Otherwise, he spotted no movement.

"Well, let's see if we can find enough salt and maybe something else that will be good to eat cold. I don't see us cooking anything in here."

Amy nodded agreement. They shouldered their packs and headed down the front stairs.

#

The gas station had a cooler filled with soda and bottled water. The cooler had long since stopped working, but the water was still good. They each grabbed several bottles. Paul looked around the store's shelves, but nothing looked edible or safe. The wrapped candy and snack food had been supplying rodents a source of food for a while now, as evidenced by seeds and chips spilling from holes gnawed in bags, boxes and wrappers—and rodent droppings.

"Yeah," Amy said pointing to the meager selection of canned foods, "none of that looks good. May not even be safe."

"I suspect we'll be limited to what we brought," Paul said. "Let's check out the cafes and restaurants."

A pizzeria and a bagel shop just a few doors down from the apartment building netted them one round container of salt. They hit the jackpot at an Italian restaurant on D Street just down the block, and a Mexican restaurant further down on the avenue. They loaded their packs with several round salt containers each.

"We can't take them all now," Paul said, hefting his pack. "But if we need more, we know where to find it."

They took their haul back to the apartment and stacked the salt rounds near the door. Then they went back out to the street. Up Third Street a couple of blocks was a market.

Inside, they found a few more bottles of water, but Paul's hopes of finding something more to eat were dashed. As they moved around, mice and rats darted around shelves and the remains of food containers.

"Okay, the whole scavenger thing isn't going to work," he said.

They found a few more undamaged salt rounds and took them, then headed back to the apartment. Paul and Amy went about the building spreading salt across doorway thresholds and window sills.

"It's going to be a long night," Paul said when they got back to the room. He pulled his tablet out of his pack and plugged it into an outlet to charge. It beeped when power connected, and Paul checked the time. "We should set a watch and get some rest before it gets dark."

Amy opened her sack lunch from the hotel.

"I will watch for a while," she said. "After you eat something, you should try to sleep. When should I wake you?"

"In about three hours," Paul said. He dug out his sack lunch and unwrapped the sandwich. "What will you do?"

"I'll read," she said, indicating her own tablet. "And keep an eye on the circle."

SIXTEEN

Hellhounds

A NEW SURVIVOR moved across the circle. Paul watched through the binoculars as it made slow progress across the brick and grass plaza. The other survivor on the far side of the circle was still there, moving in slow, shuffling steps back and forth over a fifteen-foot path.

He didn't see where the new survivor had come from. It just was there and started coming across the circle from the area of the First Street side of the station. The binoculars were pretty good and he was able to make out some of the survivor's factual features.

A chill went down his spine when the new survivor stopped and looked directly at him. He almost dropped the binoculars.

Paul checked the time on his tablet, then looked at Amy. After waking Paul, she'd dropped off to sleep almost as soon as she lay down. Her soft breathing provided a comforting background. It was full dark now, and Paul would let her sleep as long as possible.

He returned to watching the new survivor's progress across the circle. The moon and stars provided enough light for Paul to follow the new survivor easily. No other activity caught his eye. He put the binoculars down and opened the bible on his tablet. It opened to the twelfth chapter of Luke. He started reading at the twenty-second verse.

And he said to his disciples, "Therefore I tell you, do not be anxious about your life, what you will eat, nor about your body, what you will put on. For life is more than food, and the body more than clothing. Consider the ravens: they neither sow nor reap, they have neither storehouse nor barn, and yet God feeds them. Of how much more value are you than the birds! And which of you by being anxious can add a single hour to his span of life? If then you are not able to do as small a thing as that, why are you anxious about the rest?"

He looked up from the verses and smiled. He and Amy sue weren't sowing or reaping today, but God had fed them, just as He'd promised.

Father, help me to not fear, to not be anxious. I know I depend on you for so much in my life. Thank you, Jesus. Amen.

After a few minutes of meditation on the verses, he turned off the tablet and left it plugged in.

"We have a new friend out in the circle," Paul told Amy when she woke a couple of hours later.

"A friend?" she asked.

"Yes, another survivor showed up. It's on the nearer side of the circle."

He stood and stretched, then handed the binoculars to Amy.

"I see him," Amy said. "Interesting." She looked across the circle and across the front of the station. "I don't see anything else new."

"No," Paul said. "It's been uneventful, except for the new guy. We should go check the salt, though, and make sure the lines haven't been broken by rodents."

He helped her up and they grabbed some of the salt rounds.

The front door and the back door were the only entrances to the building. Thick lines of salt spread across those thresholds then across window sills and at fire escapes. Where rodent tracks disturbed the salt, Paul and Amy refreshed the lines. In the apartment they used, they spread salt on all the window sills.

Then, Paul took more salt and spread a thick line across the top of the stairs at the landing leading to the front doors, across the hall a few doors down, and then across the threshold of the apartment they were occupying.

"That should cover all our bets," he said.

They sat near the window and broke out apples and protein bars for a light, cold meal.

"They know we're here," Amy said as she cracked open a fresh water bottle. She shivered. "The new survivor looked straight at me."

Paul took a drink from his bottle and swallowed.

"He looked at me, too," he said. "I hope the salt works. I don't want any surprises."

"Do you think we're trapped here?"

"Only if we have no way out," Paul said. "I expect we'll see a hound tonight. If the salt keeps it out on the street, we can go out and face it down. If it finds a way into the building, we'll confront it, either on the stairs or down the hall." Paul waved his hand toward the other end of the hall.

"So, have you thought about how this blade, the sword, is supposed to work against a hellhound?"

"I, uh, I don't know," he said. "When we confronted the coyote, the Adversary, the sword helped me rebuke him. It hurt him, too. Whatever happened, we sent him away. Back then, I don't think the Adversary knew we had an angel blade until we rebuked him. Now he does. The demon may know, too. I don't think we can't kill the demon; we can only send him back to Hell or wherever. That's another problem all together. The hellhounds, though . . . I think we have to kill them. I don't think rebuking them will do any good."

"I agree. Killing is the only solution I can think of for the hellhounds." She chewed a piece of her protein bar, then swallowed. "I just hope you can do the job right the first time. You won't get to practice or get a do-over. Fail once, and we're both lost."

"No pressure, eh?" Paul smiled. "I don't plan to fail." To himself he thought, *No one ever plans to fail.*

They cleaned up from their meal and Paul took the trash to one of the other apartments. Amy used the bathroom while Paul went around the building checking the perimeter.

By the time Amy returned, Paul was settled near the window with his tablet and the binoculars.

"Everything looks quiet," he said. "I'll watch for a while if you want to read or relax."

Paul watched along the front of the station and checked on the survivors regularly. Their movement never changed, though every so often they seemed seemed to stop and looked at Paul. It was too dark for him to actually verify that, though. The moon moved and shadows stretched across the circle in its faint light. The stars painted a bright glow across the sky. He remembered seeing stars like this once a long time ago, when there was a huge power outage and no light pollution. Now, only an occasional street lamp was lit, and almost no other light emanated from the city. The stars were back in their glory.

Paul gazed across the circle without the binoculars and noticed a slight glow from the main entrance to the station. He reached over and gently shook Amy's shoulder.

"Something is up," he whispered. He kept his eyes on the station and got the binoculars up to take a closer look.

The entrance was empty, but a ruddy light glowed from inside the station. Flashes increased the light briefly at regular intervals. The ruddy glow grew and brightened.

Amy sat up rubbing her face and shaking out her hair.

"I think a hound is coming out," Paul whispered.

She came over to the window, pulling her hair into a ponytail and wrapping a band around it, and they both watched. The glow continued to get brighter and more red until a huge dark shape emerged from the entrance.

From their location, the shape looked vaguely like a dog. A very large dog with a huge head.

Amy shivered and Paul felt sweat trickle down his spine. He patted his vest, then reached into his pack and felt the hilt of the sword. His stomach churned and he felt his will begin to whither.

"It's just standing there," Amy said. Paul looked back out the window.

The hound swung its huge head left and right, slowly, several times. Through the binoculars, Paul could see that the head was broad, like that of a mastiff, but the snout was long and massive like a Great Dane. The ears stood up straight and pointed. A thick neck connected the head to a powerful, heavily shouldered body.

Paul's stomach churned again and his abdominal muscles fluttered.

"Father, I'm in Your hands," he said, eyes closed. "Guide me so I can do what You require. May Your will be done." The churning and fluttering stopped and he felt a warm comfort in his chest.

Amy put her hand on his shoulder.

"It's moving again," she said.

The hound made directly for the survivor on the far end of the circle.

Amy flinched as the hound started feeding on the lost soul. Paul put his arm around her and turned both of them away from the sight.

"We don't need to watch that," he said.

Amy nodded. She clung to Paul for a moment.

"All right, this is it," Paul said. "The hellhound's right there. Time for us to go after it. As long as there's just one, we should be able to confront it and kill it. Still, watch my back."

"I will," Amy said, her voice quavering. She took a deep breath and closed her eyes a moment. When she opened them, she was calmer.

Paul looked back and the hound was already moving their direction across the circle, leaving enormous tracks that burned and smoked on the bricks and grass.

SEVENTEEN

Defense

"KEEP AN EYE on the hellhound," Paul said. "I'm going to check around the building."

Paul left the room and checked the perimeter from the top floor windows. He didn't find any other glowing apparitions or burning tracks.

"It looks like this is the only one, right now," Paul said when he returned to Amy's side.

Outside, the hound had stopped at the nearer survivor for another meal and was now looking around, as it had at the front door of the station. Now that it was closer, Paul could see it was about six or seven feet at the shoulder. The huge head was ponderous as it swung left and right.

It paused, then, and the head turned. It looked straight at the window behind which Amy and Paul sat. After a moment, it turned its body and started walking slowly their direction. The head lowered and it snuffed the ground, then it moved more quickly toward their building.

At the front door, they could hear the hound snuffling around. Paul held his breath. Would the line of salt keep the hound away?

It did. After what seems a long time, the hound continued around the northwest side, under their window, and to the back. There it stopped again, evidently encountering the other line of salt there.

The hound moved back along the side under their window, its burning tracks leaving a lit trail.

About halfway along the side of the building, it stopped and backed up a bit. It seemed to be eyeing one of the windows on the ground floor. Paul and Amy hadn't put a salt barrier there.

The hound froze for a moment, focused on the window, then launched itself at the glass. It was too large to fit through the window, so it took out most of the wall as well. Flames and smoke poured from around the hole where the window had been as the hound ignited its surroundings.

"Okay, it's going to come up either the back stairs or the front stairs," Paul said. He reached into his pack and grabbed the sword. When he pulled it out of the sheath, it was glowing blue with a spiritual flame flickering around it.

Paul and Amy quietly moved out into the hall. They could hear the hound crashing through the ground floor of the building. It was moving to the back. More crashing noises followed. Then they saw the hound's glow coming from the back stairs down the hall.

The building was an older one that had been remodeled in the recent past. The hallway was still narrow, though, and the ceiling was only about nine feet high.

"This is going to be a huge advantage for us," Paul whispered. "That hellhound isn't going to have a lot of room to maneuver."

The hound appeared at the other end of the hall, its bulk completely filling the space. As it forced its way through, doors and walls gave way with sickening crunches and snaps. Crushed drywall and broken two-by-fours burst into flame around its massive shoulders and head. Paul recognized the rotten-egg odor of sulfur. Being the hound's haunches, he could see a whip-like tail lashing from side to side thumping against the walls in the narrow hallway.

A red glow emanated from the hound's dark shape, and its eyes glowed red. Paul tightened his grip on his sword. As the beast approached, the blade glowed brighter and blue flames licked out toward the beast.

The hound stopped short of the line of salt. It opened its massive jaws and spewed forth a horrible stench of sulfur and death. Paul's stomach twisted and his eyes brimmed with tears.

Then the hound spoke, in a booming, impossibly deep voice. "I come for you," a it said.

"Fat chance, hellhound," Paul said, showing more bravado than he actually felt. He sensed Amy at his back, staff at the ready to defend him.

"I come for you," the voice boomed again. The hound made a step toward the salt line, then pulled back. "You must come."

Paul stepped toward the hound, holding the sword before him. The sword's brilliance increased as the flames leapt and lashed at the hound. The hound flinched but stood its ground.

"Come," it said. The head turned and the jaws snapped at Paul, but it could not cross the line of salt.

Paul moved closer. The sword now vibrated with energy, and the blue light was almost blinding. The flames licked at the hound's head. Whimpering, the hound drew back.

By now Paul had almost reached the salt line.

"You serve an evil master," Paul yelled at the hound. "You will never have me or Amy."

The flames of the sword bathed the hound with blue brilliance. The hound tried to back away, lowering its head almost to the floor. The narrow hallway restricted the beast's movement, but flames started consuming the walls.

Paul leaped across the line of salt and stabbed down on the hound's head with the sword.

A tremendous howl reverberated through the building. The bulky body of the hound collapsed on the floor, and its red glow from the hound faded.

Paul pulled the sword from the hounds head, then stabbed again behind the shoulders, hoping to hit the heart.

Blue flame shot through the hound and out its eyes, mouth, and feet. Paul struggled to pull the sword out, bracing his feet against the head, and it finally came free. Pieces of the hound's flesh and blood burned off the blade and fell away.

Sulfurous smoke wafted through the hall, and small fires burned on the walls and floor.

Amy covered her mount and nose against the fumes. Coughing, she said, "I don't think we should stay here."

"Yeah," Paul agreed. "Let's pack up and get out."

They hurried back to the apartment and they looked toward the station. All was dark, with no sign of another hound. Of course, that didn't mean another hound hadn't come out while they were fighting this one. But the first hound had eaten all the food, the survivors. That hound's flaming tracks were now just smoldering, with little black wisps of smoke rising into the night.

Paul scanned with the binoculars to see if there were any fresher flaming tracks near the front of the station. He didn't see anything new.

"Okay, I think we're good," he said. "We'd better hurry, though. The fire's spreading down he hall, and the top floor will be filled with smoke before long."

Buy the time they'd finished packing, heavier smoke was coming from the far stairway. They put the rest of the salt rounds in some fabric grocery sacks and made their way to the front entrance. The rear of the building was fully engulfed in flames, and smoke poured down the lower hall.

They made it across the street to a sidewalk next to a little triangle park. For a moment they stood watching the fire consume the apartment building. Paul half expected to hear a fire engine siren.

"Where should we go?" Amy asked.

"Let's go that way," Paul said, pointing west. "There are some places there where we can keep a close eye on the station and the circle, and be safe for the rest of the night."

"Oh, I remember a college or university building over there," Amy said. "That would be a good vantage."

They headed down D Street, keeping close to the trees lining the sidewalk. It was pretty dark, but Paul didn't want to take any chances. There could be spies or lookouts around.

As they walked, the apartment building became completely engulfed in flames, and the fire spread to an adjacent building. The breeze blew most of the smoke to the northeast, but they could hear, a couple blocks away, the buildings burning and collapsing.

"Ohio State University?" Paul said as they approached the building facing North Capitol Street NW. "Kinda out of place, isn't it? Ohio's a couple of states over."

"Yeah," Amy said. "That's why I remember it. The name stuck out."

They found an entrance to the north wing, went inside, and left a line of salt across the doorway. A broad staircase led up, and they found a large bank of windows on the east end of the building in the upper floor.

Paul moved to the wall of windows and looked out over the circle. A glow from the fire cast strange, moving shadows across the parks and the circle.

Suddenly, the ground shuddered and an explosion rocked the center.

"What was that?" Amy asked.

"Looks like the fire in the apartment building spread to the gas station next door," Paul replied. "The fuel left in the storage tanks exploded."

The windows of their building wobbled and shook but didn't break.

"We're lucky those windows didn't shatter," Amy said.

"No kidding."

Paul got the binoculars out and looked toward the fire. All the rest of the buildings in the oddly shaped block were involved in the fire now.

"I hope I don't get in trouble for this," he said. "It wasn't my fault."

Amy gave him a wry grin. "I don't think this counts as arson, and even if it did, there aren't any police left to arrest you."

The area next to the windows had long lounges and soft chairs. Paul and Amy set up their camp and kept watch over the front of Union Station and the circle. Nothing moved the rest of the night. Paul took the first watch. Around dawn, he woke Amy and took his turn sleeping.

#

Paul woke to filtered sunlight coming through the large windows. Smoke still rose from the burnt-out buildings on the other side of the circle, but the fire hadn't spread any further. Amy sat in a chair on watch with the binoculars hung around her neck.

"Some survivors came out," she said. "They're around the station now. One came from First Street, over there, and another came from across the way."

Paul looked where Amy pointed. "Probably sent here by the fallen as meals for another hellhound," he said. "Which means we'll have another hound to face tonight. But before that happens, I need to brush my teeth."

He got out some of this toiletries and headed to the restrooms. After he came back, Amy took her turn in the restrooms.

Paul used the binoculars to see what the buildings looked like around the apartment they'd used last night. The whole block had burned to the ground. Steel ribs of the building skeletons poked up from the smoking rubble. Other than that, nothing was left standing. Fortunately, the streets were keeping the fire contained in the odd-shaped block.

"Good thing that fire wasn't your fault," Amy said, returning from the restrooms. "That block was probably worth hundreds of millions of dollars."

"Don't rub it in," he said. "It was the hellhound's fault. Send Satan the bill."

"He'd probably weasel his way out of it," Amy said.

Paul looked around the area from their vantage.

"I doubt we can find another site like the apartment building," he said. "This may be our best bet. At least this building probably won't burn to the ground afterward."

Amy looked around.

"We should probably move some of the furniture, then make a circle of salt out over there," she said, pointing about ten feet out. "That gives us a little room to move around."

They shifted the chairs and lounges closer to the walls then poured a line of salt in a large arc across the room. They set up camp near the window until night. Then they prepared to meet the next hound.

EIGHTEEN

Fight

THEY SCOUTED the nearby restaurants and stores for anything to add to their food and water supply. Paul found a new pair of shoes. They then returned to the room with the wall of windows.

While they'd been foraging, three more survivors had showed up in the circle.

"That doesn't bode well," Paul said. Looking through the binoculars, he counted again to make sure. "Yep, six."

"The other hound ate two survivors before attacking us," Amy said. "This could mean three hounds?"

"If we had any sense," Paul said, "we'd pack up and run now."

He looked around the room and at the nearby area below the window.

"We're too high for them to jump through the windows from the street. And the salt will keep them far enough away we can harass and pick at them one at a time."

Amy looked around. "I think the 'run now' part is my favorite choice."

"But we really don't have a choice," Paul said. "We're in it to win it. We're God's soldiers."

"I know," she said with a sigh. "That was just weakness talking."

"You're not weak, Amy. You've been incredibly strong through this whole ordeal, and your strength has helped me more than you'll ever know. You've just got to be strong a little longer."

She smiled. "Thanks, Paul."

Then she looked at her staff and started walking around the perimeter and the salt line, shifting some of the chairs and lounges again to clear the area. She looked at Paul thoughtfully for a moment.

When she turned back to the line of salt, she started moving with the staff. It spun and twirled in her hands, thrusting against imaginary opponents and making head-cracking sweeps. Her feet stepped along inside the line of salt without disturbing it.

Paul watched her moved across the room. Sometimes her movements looked like ballet, sometimes like modern dance, but always with a point of attack. The staff was an extension of her arms and legs. For one move, she leapt from the center of the room, using the staff, wheeling and almost touching the ceiling, then landed on the other side of the room, just inside the salt line.

Precise and fluid, Paul thought. *A deadly art.*

Amy continued to practice for about half an hour, then paused to rest and catch her breath. Leaning on her staff, she looked deep in thought. Then she started a new set of lunges, attacks, parries, and leaps. She moved one direction, leapt and pivoted with the staff, and changed direction. She used her feet to kick, then follow with the staff for more bone-cracking blows.

"Remind me to never get you angry," Paul said when she finished.

She smiled and lifted the staff. "Just don't get me angry with this in my hands."

She went to her pack and got out toiletries and fresh clothes. "I'm all sweaty. I'm going to clean up."

While she was gone, Paul sat thinking about their fights during the Troubles. At one point he used the sword in one hand and the staff in the other. But here, with the hellhounds, he figured that the sword alone was his best shot. If there were three hounds tonight, the fight would be tough. With Amy working her staff and drawing attention, Paul could focus on getting at one hound at a time.

He took out his sword and moved to the line of salt. His hand wrapped around the hilt in a perfect, comfortable, controlled grip. In the light of day with no hound nearby, the blade didn't glow blue. It was still beautiful, though, clean and shining, and tapering out to the tip in a smooth, graceful, balanced shape.

Last night the sword flame had backed the hound away. Paul could use that to open his advantage on one hound, buying himself time to move around and strike. He would have to leap across the salt, attack, and leap back before the hound, or another hound, could counterattack. The hound's size and mass would make it difficult to find a single strike point. In addition, it would probably use that huge head, neck, and tail as weapons.

Paul worked around an imaginary hound, trying moves and thrusts, avoiding disturbing the line of salt. He needed to find a way through to a heart stab, without being caught in a hound's jaws or between two hounds. Two possible areas were under the chest and, as last night, over the back and behind the shoulders. Bone did not seem to deflect the sword, as the stab into the head had demonstrated. If he went under and between the front legs, with a slash against the neck, followed by a thrust up into the chest, that might work as well.

He practiced those moves and worked up his own sweat. By the time Amy came out of the restrooms he was breathing hard and his shirt was soaked.

"My turn," he said. He put away the sword and took off the vest. He hung the vest on a chair to air out, then got his toiletries and some fresh clothes and went to the restrooms.

He came back to the windows feeling much better. Amy was scanning the circle with the binoculars.

"Anything new?" he asked.

"No. Just the six survivors. But they all stopped and stared at us. So we can assume they—the hounds and the demon—know where we are."

Paul put his vest back on, then got out some of their food.

"A cold dinner," he said handing her an apple and a protein bar. She reached into her pack and pulled out a baggie of cookies.

"I've been saving these."

They were chocolate chip and must have been baked at the hotel.

He laughed and blessed the meal.

After they ate and washed it all down with their room-temperature water, Paul cleaned up the cores and wrappers, then checked the line of salt around their camp area.

"I'll watch first," he said. "You go ahead and take a rest. It'll be getting dark soon."

Amy nodded, then stretched out on top of her sleeping bag that was spread out on one of the lounges. She read from her tablet for a few minutes and fell asleep. Paul gently put her tablet away and set up to read and watch the circle.

As they day faded, Paul woke Amy so he could nap.

"Wake me as soon as anything happens," he said.

"Don't worry," she said. "I will."

#

"Wake up, Paul," she whispered, nudging his shoulder. It seemed he'd just dozed off. "It's starting."

He sat up, shook his head a bit, then reached for a water bottle and took a drink.

They watched out the window as the ruddy glow from the station front increased. The six survivors continued their slow, shuffling march back and forth.

"Think we're ready to handle three?" Paul asked.

"It'll be a little dicey," Amy said. "All one has to do is get hold of one of us and that'll be it. I'd rather it be just one, or two."

"Me, too," he agreed. "Still, we should be able to work together on this and win."

"You're such an optimist, Paul."

The glow from the station grew brighter. A dark form appeared as they watched. Amy had the binoculars and gasped as the hound fully appeared.

"It's a female," she said. "And she's had puppies!"

She handed the binoculars to Paul. Amy was right: the hound was a mother. He could see the dugs handing from her abdomen. He watched as the hound moved into the circle. It stood, wagging its head from side to side, sniffing the air. Then it moved toward one of the survivors. Behind it was other movement coming through the door. This time it was Paul's turn to gasp.

"We don't have three adult hounds, this time," Paul said. "She has four puppies following her."

He lowered the binoculars and looked at Amy. "We'll be facing five hounds."

He looked through the binoculars again. The puppies were about one fourth the size of the mother and scampered around the circle looking for survivors to eat. The adult hound finished the one survivor and moved to another. The puppies each found one and started feeding.

Paul silently handed the binoculars to Amy. She watched a while, then set down the binoculars.

"Oh, this is horrible. Puppies! I love puppies. For that matter, I love dogs. But these . . . creatures . . . yuck!"

"I know. They aren't like real dogs at all. I mean, they look like dogs and act like dogs, but not in a way that makes them the least bit lovable. They're like a perversion of what a dog ought to be."

"And they feast on human flesh," Amy added. "Yeah, I'm not going to feel bad about killing them."

She took another look. "Those puppies move pretty fast. If we attack them first, the mother will come in to defend them. If we attack the mother first, the puppies will likely swarm us. They may be smaller, but they're still big enough to drag us out."

She looked at Paul. "Tell me they can't really drag us to Hell."

"I doubt it," he said. "We are God's children, after all. William just spouted the lies the demon fed him. That doesn't mean we can't be dragged to the demon, tortured, and martyred."

"I'm going to do my best to see that we don't get dragged anywhere."

"We're going to have to be fast and not give either the mother or the puppies a chance to be effective," Paul said. "If you make feints against the puppies, kind of attract their attention, that may distract the mother enough I can get a quick kill. Then we can move against the puppies."

"Might work," she said.

They watched as the hound and her pups finished feeding and started moving toward their building. The adult hound moved with sure, steady steps. The puppies bounded around, generally following their mother.

When they got to North Capitol Street, the hound looked up at the wall of windows for a moment, then led her puppies to the entrance. Paul and Amy couldn't see what happened then, but they guessed that the line of salt across the door blocked them. But the mother hound just crashed through a large ground-floor window. The sulfur smell rose into the room as the hound and pups started climbing the stairs.

The ruddy glow filled the other side of the room as the hounds arrived. Paul, sword in hand, moved to the line of salt on their right. Amy, staff spinning, moved to the line on the left.

The hound came to the line of salt near the center, with puppies on either side.

Paul's sword's blue glow grew to a blinding level and the flames licked out at the hounds, causing the nearer ones to yip and whimper. On a hunch, Paul jabbed the sword at the two puppies on his side, and the flames roared out of the sword, bathing the pups in blue light.

The pups ran to the other side of their mother yipping and crying. The adult hound came at Paul in a rush, jaws snapping. The death-like, sulfurous breath wafted at him. Paul thrust the sword at the hound's snout and the blue flames bathed its head. In its rush to get away, the hound slipped on the smooth floor, stumbled, and fell.

Paul took advantage of the moment and jumped across the line of salt, swinging the sword against the hound's exposed neck as it rolled across the room. The sword bit, slashing across the throat. Black blood gushed from the wound. Paul jumped again, leaping across the flailing legs, and stabbed the sword deep into the hound's chest. As before, blue light flooded the inside of the beast and came out its eyes, mouth and feet. An anguished howl echoed across the circle and out into the night.

Paul stood and turned. The hound's blood covered him, but it was already burning off, the blue glow from his sword spreading through his body.

Amy kept the smaller hounds involved by jumping back and forth across the salt line, cracking heads and ribs with the staff. The puppies weren't as exuberant now that their mother was dead, but suddenly acquired a more evil and bloodthirsty presence.

Paul, still on the other side of the salt, came at the pups from the flank, sword flaming and glowing. The first pup to attack him lost its head to a swing of the sword. Amy jumped across again, whacking a pup's head. Its head bounced against the floor and the pup stumbled around, dazed. She jumped back as the other two tried to attack her.

Paul came in and stabbed another pup in the chest. A small howl and a flash of blue light signaled the pup's demise. It was almost pitiful, but not really.

Two pups remained, Paul dispatched the dazed pup, then decapitated the last one just after Amy cracked its ribs.

They moved away from the hounds and looked at their work.

The decapitated pups continued to jerk and twitch. Paul nodded, then went to each and stabbed them in the heart. That finished them.

A blue glow flowed through Paul. On impulse, he touched Amy's hand, and the glow passed to her as well. Hound remains and blood burned off, leaving Paul and Amy clean. The blue glow faded, and the sword went back to its normal steel sheen..

Paul got on his knees and prayed.

"Father, thank You for Your grace and the wisdom and strength to do Your work. I say this in Your Son's Name, Jesus Christ. Amen."

"Amen," Amy repeated. "Amen."

The bodies of the hounds left a sulfurous odor, and there were some smoldering bits lying about.

"We can't stay," Amy said. "Let's head back to the high school."

Paul nodded. They packed up their gear.

The night passage back to the high school was slow. They paused often to watch for movement in the side streets. Sometimes, they simply stopped on the porch of a row house and rested. Paul would hold Amy while she napped, then she would hold him while he napped. They reached the high school just as dawn began breaking, with the sun peaking under clouds that signaled rain.

NINETEEN

Redemption

GARY WELCOMED them into the gym and made sure they got a hot breakfast, then settled them into cots in one of the classrooms. They slept most of the day.

Later, after they got up and showered, Brad and Janet arrived.

"We need a report," Brad said. "There are all kinds of rumors and wild speculation spreading around. We heard an explosion and saw the fire. What happened?"

"Yeah, we sort of blew up a gas station," Paul said.

"*What?*" said Janet.

"Well, I don't see how we can be held responsible for the explosion," said Amy. "We didn't even start the fire. The hellhound did that."

"Maybe you'd better start at the beginning," said Brad.

Paul and Amy told them what had happened, and what they's seen. After they reached the end, Brad and Janet sat back and looked at each other a moment.

"You killed six hellhounds?" Brad said, at last.

Paul shrugged. "We were just lucky."

"What happened here?" asked Amy.

"It was pretty wild," Janet said, "but not as wild as what happened to you two."

"Yeah," Brad said. "See, we had the idea we would watch the bridges where the salt barriers were, just to see if the hounds ever came along. We had teams on each of the sites, all with the new rifles the four of us found in the Senate Office building that day.

"After full dark, these red, glowing hounds started crossing the bridges. They got up to the salt and stopped. We opened fire. They just stood there. We could see the bullets going in to the hounds but they had no impact. The hounds just stared at us."

"But, then," Janet said, "all of a sudden, they looked toward the northeast, where you guys were. There was a mournful howl, and the hellhounds turned and left. It wasn't long after that we heard the explosion and saw the huge fireball from your gas station explosion."

"How many hounds did you see at the bridges?" Amy asked.

"We think there may have been five, all together," Brad said. "They came back the next night. Same drill as before: they made it as far as the salt, we opened fire, and the bullets had no effect. Then, at one point they all looked in your direction and sat on their haunches and whined and howled. Then they left."

"Five full-grown hounds, eh?" Paul said. He looked at Amy.

"We'll need to figure out a way to get them separated," Amy said. "We might be able to fight two, maybe three, at a time. But no way we could win against five at once."

"Maybe we should use the bridges," Brad said. "We get you back to the hotel tonight, then set up teams at the bridges again. When the hounds show up, we bring you to one of the bridges. Divide and conquer."

"That's a good plan," Paul said. "But before we get out of here, Amy and I should check in with Daryll and William."

Paul and Amy found Daryll and chatted with him for a bit. Daryll was progressing well and had become a full member of the team at the site. He helped clean up new survivors, fed them, talked to them and even participated in some conversions. They found that Daryll was just one of several survivors who made a full recovery and experienced salvation. Those fully recovered survivors stayed within the confines of the site, though, just in case the demon had other resources.

When they found William, he wept openly and begged their help. He could feel the death of the hounds when Paul killed them, and knew the rage of the demon.

"Please, break my final bonds with Nelchael," he pleaded. "I know he lied. Help me find forgiveness and Jesus."

Paul gathered as many free helpers as possible, got out his sword and started a chain of prayers over William. The sword glowed blue as the participants prayed and it finally came to Paul.

"Father, we come to You for Your grace and support and ask that You remove the hold this demon has on William," he said. "Please help William come back to You as a repentant son and accept Jesus as his Lord and Savior. In the name of Your Son, Jesus Christ, remove this demon's hold on William now! Begone, demon!"

The blue flame flowed into William, glowing out of his eyes and even the ends of his hair. When it winked out and William shook, then opened his eyes.

"I'm free," he said.

"If you are ready, then," Paul said, "say this prayer. Father, I come to You as a sinner and confess my sins. I want to live my life for You, now. I repent and ask Your forgiveness."

William repeated the prayer.

"I believe You sacrificed Yourself on the cross to pay for my sins. You did what I could not do. I come to You now and give You my life. Help me live it as would please You."

William repeated again.

"Amen."

"Amen," William said. He looked up, his eyes bright, and smiled. "I can feel God!"

"Good," Paul said. "Amy and I have to leave, but the pastor and the others here will help you with prayer and comfort. Know now, William, that you are a child of God. God loves you and so does everyone here."

Paul and Amy said their goodbyes around the gym, then left with Brad and Janet.

"We'll be at the hotel in plenty of time to give the elder an update before the evening reports," Brad said as he drove away from the high school. "He'll be glad to see you two."

#

"That's quite a tale," Elder Franklin said after Paul and Amy gave him a complete report of their activities. "And, I don't mean to discount anything you said by that."

"We understand, Elder Franklin," Amy said. "We were in it and I still have trouble believing what happened."

"Anyway," Paul said, "Brad suggested that we set things up at the bridges and call us in to dispatch a hound when they show up. We can probably take out two tonight, if we work quickly."

"Yes, I understand," the elder said. "Let's hear the reports when they come in and see if anything changes. Go see your families for a bit, then come down when the teams come back."

#

"The sites at Cardozo and Banneker have a pretty good perimeter of salt laid," one team member said at the evening reports. "They each had a hellhound or two come around each night, some at the same time we confronted those on the bridges. They came around again last night and prowled for quite a while, then left near dawn."

"We had five show up at the bridges last night," the elder said, "so we now we think there might be at least seven. How are the sites holding up with the hounds coming around at night?"

"Doing well, considering. Those hounds are huge and frightening, and some of the staff at the sites probably need to rotate out or we may have some breakdowns."

"Noted," the elder said. "Any other reports?"

No one spoke up.

"In that case," the elder said, "we think we have a plan to start taking out the rest of these hounds."

He explained how they will again put teams on each of the bridges, refresh the salt lines, and watch for the hounds.

"When they come, we'll bring Paul and Amy to one of the bridges," the else said. "To limit our risk, though, we only want Paul and Amy to face one or two hounds at a time. If only one shows up at a bridge, that is the bridge we will have them come to. We may get two hounds killed a night this way." He waved his hand at some of the voices raising questions. "Wait a moment. They have killed six hounds so far."

That brought the crowd to silence.

"Two adults and four puppies," Amy said.

"Puppies?" a dark-haired man in the audience said loudly. "Puppies?"

"We think the first one was a male," Paul said. "And the second adult was obviously female and had a brood of pups with her."

"So, back to the plan," the elder said. "Killing two hounds in a night may not be the most productive, but it is the most effective use of our limited hound-killing resource. This will take several days. Once the hounds are gone, we have a demon to hunt down."

The man who spoke earlier raised his hand. Elder Franklin acknowledged him.

"We've used high-powered firearms against the hounds," he said, "and nothing seems to hurt them. I guess I don't understand how a kid kills them."

Paul stood and pulled the sword out of its sheath in the backpack. He held it up, rolling his wrist a little to let the light flash on the blade. "This is what I used."

"You have to get pretty close to stick those horrible hounds with that," the man said. "Pardon me if I have trouble believing you."

"It's hard to explain," Paul said, slipping the sword back in its sheath. "But, over the next couple nights, you'll see how it works."

"How many of those do you have?" the man asked. "Are you sure one of us wouldn't be better using that sword?"

"Just the one," the elder answered. "And, just the one special young man to wield it."

#

"We're ready," Brad said into the hand-held radio, "over."

Evening light faded quickly and the rifle teams were already stationed at the bridges. It was now just a matter of waiting. Paul and Amy sat in the back seats of Brad's crossover, holding their staffs. Paul had the sword in its sheath, with a strap that would go around his waist.

They left their packs back at the hotel.

"I'm a little worried," Amy said. "I just realized I won't know the area we'll be working in. How far can I jump? How much room do I have to move?"

"You'll be fine," Paul said. "You'll keep to my left. If I go right, you go left. We divide the hound's attention, distract him. If there are two, you keep one busy. Just don't get too close."

Brad and Janet listened from the front.

"You two work well together," Brad said. "I'd guess that as soon as you are on the bridge and confronting the hounds you'll just flow with each other."

Paul smiled, nodding. He looked at Amy, then turned to Brad.

"You should have seen her practicing before we faced the second hound and her pups. Amy's a work of art."

Amy dropped her head, letting her hair fall across and hide her face.

"And, in the fight, she was ferocious!"

"You were supposed to be paying attention to what you were doing, Paul," Amy said.

Paul gently punched her shoulder.

"I told you before," he said, "I couldn't do this without you at my side."

Amy reached across in the darkness and touched his hand.

"Just so you are there," she said.

TWENTY

Bridge Fight

THE RADIO CHIRPED.

"Brad, come in. Over."

"Brad here. Over."

"Two hounds at the salt line on Teddy Roosevelt. Over."

"Roger," Brad said. "Hold position. Over."

After a couple minutes, the radio chirped again.

"Two hounds at the line on Arlington Memorial. Over."

"Roger. Hold position. Over."

A few seconds later, another call came in.

"One hound on the US 29 bridge. Over."

"Roger," Brad said. He looked at Paul and Amy, who both nodded. "On the way. Over."

Brad spun the car around and sped down the George Washington Parkway. When he got to the bridge, he hopped the median and wound up the ramp. He brought the car to a screeching halt near the rifle team who was braced behind sand bags and facing the hound at the salt line.

Paul got out and strapped on the sword. He left his staff in the car. Amy was already at the front of the car, looking at the hound. It was alone, as far as they could see. The ruddy glow from the hound made it hard to see past it. It stood as near the salt as it dared. Its snapped its huge jaws at Amy and the others, and whipped its tail back and forth.

The ruddy glow from the hound's body lit the area, leaving weird shifting shadows dancing across the bridge. An oppressive fear radiated from the hound and Paul could see it reflected in the eyes of the team behind the sandbags.

"I shouldn't need to remind anyone that there is no shooting while Amy and I are out there," Paul said to the people holding rifles. "Right?"

They nodded.

Paul started walking toward the beast and Amy fell in to his left. The salt line looked fresh and was doing its job. Paul drew the sword.

Blue light flashed from the blade and the blue flames licked toward the hound. The hound growled and snapped its teeth at the sword. But when the blue flames flowed into its face, it backed off and whimpered.

Paul swept to the right, almost touching the salt line and jabbed with the sword at the hounds shoulder. The hound flinched and growled in pain as the blue flames bathed its left leg.

Amy jumped across the line of salt, staff spinning, and cracked down on the hound's right foot. She jumped back across the salt just before the tail came sweeping around in a fiery red blur.

The hound's head swept across toward Amy, snapping its jaws and growling. It lifted its left leg to step, and Paul moved across the salt. The sword thrust flame ahead of itself, and Paul stabbed up under the left leg and deep into that side of the chest. At the same time, Amy's staff came across the jaws of the hound, slapping it hard enough to slam the head against its right shoulder.

The hound went down with a tremendous howl that reverberated across the bridge, with intense blue light blazing from its eyes, mouth, and feet.

Paul pulled the sword out of the hound as it died, blood pouring from the punctured lung and heart. The blue flame burned off the remains of the hound from itself and Paul, then the blue light winked out. Paul put the sword back in its sheath.

Amy and Paul walked back to the car.

"We messed up the salt line," Paul said. "Hope you have some more."

One of the women in the rifle team shook her head. Brad got in the back of the car and tossed her a small bag of salt. She immediately went to refresh the line.

Brad's radio chirped.

"This is the Teddy Roosevelt. One of the hounds left. We only have one hound, now. Over."

Brad looked at Paul and Amy. They nodded.

"On the way," Brad said into the radio. "Over."

When everyone was in the car, Brad drove back down the parkway.

#

Paul and Amy worked the hound on the Theodore Roosevelt Memorial Bridge in a similar way. Paul directed the flames of the sword to harass the hound, while Amy feinted and spun her staff to distract it. Paul dove under the hound's front legs for the final thrust through the heart and was rewarded with a bath in the hound's blood.

The sword's blue flame cleansed him and winked out.

"That's a pretty nice feature of the sword, how it cleans all the blood and bits of flesh from itself and you," Amy said.

"Yeah," said Paul. "I'm glad I don't have to walk around covered in all that much, or deal with cleaning it."

As Paul and Amy came back to the car, Brad took reports from the other bridges. The hounds all left. The teams refreshed the salt lines and set up to wait for their watch relief later in the night.

Brad drove the team back to the hotel. Paul sat in the back seat unbuckling the sword and wrapping the strap around the sheath.

"We took two down, tonight," Amy said. "That means there should only be five left, at most."

"Assuming there really were just seven," Janet said. "There could be a couple more or a couple less."

"Yeah, I heard there are so many of the hellhound trails in and out of Foggy Bottom, the whole area is scorched and there's no way to figure out how many there are," Brad said. "When we check in with the Eastern, Cardozo and Banneker sites tomorrow, we'll find out if any hounds showed up tonight."

"If none showed at the sites," Paul said, "the five that showed at the bridges are it. We killed two. There should be three left. That's what I'll be praying for tonight."

Janet watched Paul over the seat.

"When that sword glows," she said, "do you know your whole body glows?"

Paul looked at her a moment.

"No," he said. "I'm too busy to worry about that."

"Yeah," she said. "And when the flames come out, you just radiate. Can you feel it?"

"I feel focused. That's about all. But when the light winks out, I feel kind of alone."

#

They slept late and grabbed a light breakfast before meeting with the elder. He prayed over them, and they shared the results of the previous night.

"We'll know more about how many hounds are left by tonight," Elder Franklin said. "But that's not what's on my mind today. When we clear the hounds, we need to find this demon. We can't kill a demon. It is an immortal being, like an angel. If there is a way to kill a demon, we humans don't have the means to do so. But with God's help and the authority of Jesus Christ, we can cast the demon down, expel it from this plane of existence. We can send it back to wherever Satan lives."

"Isn't that hell?" Amy asked.

"That's a point of controversy," the elder said. "Satan and his followers were cast out of heaven; the Bible makes that much clear. Some believe they were sent to Earth, but in a spiritual plane. According to this line of thought, Satan and the fallen will be cast into hell after the future return of Jesus Christ. Others believe Satan and the fallen were cast into the lake of fire, or hell, after being run out of heaven in the first place. The passages in the ancient texts not specific on this and leave it open to interpretation."

"So, all we need to do is cast out the demon?" Paul asked.

"I doubt it will be that simple," the elder said. "We have to bring authority to send this Nelchael back into Satan's realm. We have the Holy Bible," he put his hand on the Bible on his desk, "and we have ordained ministers. I'm just a lay leader, so I don't know if my faith would hold enough authority."

"What do you mean?" Paul asked.

"Well, being a follower of Jesus gives a person authority over demons, but it isn't a simple matter of every Christian being able to instantly send any demon packing just by saying the word. There seem to be degrees of authority involved, and some demons appear to be more stubborn than others. Even Jesus seems to have had some difficulty in getting certain demons to leave. Early in His ministry He rebuked Satan directly, and Satan left Him alone for the time being. But after that Satan seems to have dogged Him off and on right up to the end. Maybe that was just part of the limitation Jesus took by living in the form of a mortal man.

"I've been studying the passages in the Bible where Jesus and His disciples drove out demons, trying to make sense of it all. Most of the demons cast out by the disciples were what I might call small ones—troublesome and wicked, but small. Jesus met one that called itself Legion, and the lore indicates Legion was one of the really big demons, or it might have been a lot of demons working together. Jesus was able to send Legion away on his own, though it took him a while."

The elder rubbed his hands on his face and took a deep breath.

"Another place in the New Testament talks about a group who cast out demons in the name of Jesus Christ, but didn't actually know Jesus or have authority through Him. They got caught by a tough demon, it seems, and they got trashed."

"We don't have that problem, anyway," Paul said. "We do know Jesus"

"Yes. We have some authority, but as I said, it's not that simple and I'm not entirely certain how we proceed."

Paul considered the elders words.

"Once we start hunting the demon down in the underground," Amy said, "the hellhounds won't be our only worry. William said that Nelchael has other help. He didn't specify what that was."

"Then," Paul said, "we should have another talk with William. He's fully converted and saved. We should be able to get more detail from him now."

"Excellent idea," the elder said. He gathered up his Bible and keys. "I'll drive."

Paul and Amy gathered their packs and staffs and followed the elder out.

"I've been wanting to get out here for a while, anyway," the elder said as he drove toward Eastern High School.

#

They found Gary right away at the high school, and hustled the elder into the gym while he held his hand over his nose and mouth.

"The odor's a bit bad this morning," Gary said by way of apology. "We just brought in a truck with eight survivors. It's much better inside."

Paul and Amy got some coffee while Gary introduced the elder to some of the saved survivors. They even got to chat with Daryll for a few minutes. Then they found William and sat at one of the tables.

William was bright and smiling, and seemed full of an energy he didn't have before.

"Thank you so much for helping me find Jesus," he said immediately. "I'm learning to have a relationship with God and I know I've had the Holy Spirit. I've needed so much healing."

"I'm glad for you," Paul said. "We've been praying for you."

"I hear you are pretty busy, too," William said.

"That's why we're here," Paul said. "This is Elder Franklin, our mission leader."

"Pleased to meet you, William," the elder said.

"Very happy to meet you, elder."

"William, we need to find out all you know about the demon, Nelchael, and what resources he has. I know this is a tough subject for you, but any information you can give us will help."

"I'm sorry to tell you, he has an army of survivors surrounding him. Even if you kill all the hellhounds, you will still need to fight through the survivors to reach him."

"Survivors like we've been gathering?" Amy asked.

"No, these are special survivors," William said. "Like me, they were cared for and convinced he would rule them. They will be used to protect him. They can fight. He never intended those survivors as food for the hounds. And, he has some imps—small troublesome demons."

"But he has hold of those special survivors like he did with you, right?" Paul said.

"Yes," William said. "You won't be able to turn them when you find them. They will be to close too him. You'll have to fight."

"But if they die there," Amy said, "their souls will be lost."

William nodded. "Yes. But if you don't face him, he'll only get stronger. More souls will be lost if he isn't stopped."

"So," the elder said, "what does this demon fear?"

"He fears your mission," William said. "He fears Paul and Amy. I used to think he was unbeatable, but now I realize now that his hold on this plane is tenuous. When the black fog came down Satan brought him to this place to rule and torment. Since the fog lifted and Satan left him alone here, he knows he's in danger. If he can't deliver Paul and Amy, Nelchael will suffer at the hands of Satan."

TWENTY-ONE

Storm

"THOSE FIREARMS from the Senate Office building were a lucky find," Elder Franklin said as they drove back to the hotel. "We have to get to Nelchael, and we will have to go through those survivors to do it."

"My heart breaks for those poor souls," Amy said, tears forming in her eyes. "I wish there were a way to save even a few of them."

"Well, we won't be able to touch them," Paul said. "If they're anything like the survivors we've gathered, we'll lose any of our people who make skin-to-skin contact with them."

"William said they'll fight," the elder said. "He didn't say they would have weapons. I wonder."

They rode in silence the rest of the trip to the hotel.

#

"Evidently," Brad said at the evening report meeting, "no hounds showed up around the sites last night. Based on that, we're guessing we probably have just the three hounds left to fight."

"As far as the hounds go, that is," Elder Franklin said. "Once they are out of the way, we have some other challenges to face. I want to work with all of you who are combat vets," he nodded to Brad and James Carson, "to figure out a plan for when we go into the tunnels. We'll need to go in fully armed and ready to fight."

Elder Franklin explained what they probably faced in the tunnels, based on the information provided by William, the former Senator.

"This is going to be a tough fight," the elder said. "And, we'll be escorting civilians—our pastors, myself, and Paul and Amy. They must be brought to the final confrontation with the demon."

#

Elder Franklin and a handful of vets met for an hour afterward and then the vets left to gather people. Paul and Amy waited in the hotel lobby as activity and excitement increased throughout the hotel. They would still confront the hounds that evening at the bridges, but others were preparing for a different kind of action.

"We should try to think about how to take two adult hounds at once," Amy said. "I doubt we can take one at a time tonight and get all three."

"Assuming there are only three left," Paul said.

"I'm wondering about that, too," Amy said. "Let's go outside and do a little practice."

They found a couple of abandoned cars parked in a nearby parking lot, spaced about as far apart as they would expect two hounds to be.

"So far," Paul said, "these have been pretty simple. Distract the beast, hit it with the sword's flame, go under its defense, and strike. With the pups, you were able to distract the hound by whacking the little ones. I came in under her guard and killed her.

"With two adults, though, we won't have one trying to protect the other. If we distract one, the other will try to attack one of us. You should be able to keep one hound's attention without crossing the salt by whacking it on the head with your staff. The other hound, I'll have to hit with the flame, jump across, stab, jump back, move, and repeat until I can make an opening for a kill."

They practiced the suggested moves against the cars, with Paul using a branch in place of the sword. Amy put a number of dents into the hood of the car on the left as she worked some new ideas into her routine. They worked on moving together, setting a rhythm to their attacks and feints.

"That should work," Paul said, breathing heavily after a half-hour practicing. Daylight was fading. "We better get back to the lobby and see who will take us around to the bridges."

#

Brad drove them out to the bridges again, this time without Janet. She stayed behind to help prepare for the next phase, after the hounds were killed.

By the time they got to the banks of the Potomac on the parkway, it was full dark and the radio chatter started. All the bridge watches checked in, with no sightings of hounds, yet.

They sat and watched the stars reflecting on the dark, muddy waters of the river. Paul sat quietly, thumbing the hilt of his sword. Amy hummed a hymn. Brad held the radio. He checked the back seat every once in a while, as if making sure Paul and Amy were still there.

"We're still here," Paul said at last. "I don't think we could sneak out of the back seat without you noticing."

Brad smiled. "I guess I'm a little antsy and tired of waiting around. Now that we're ready, I just want to get it over with."

Just them the radio came to life, and they all jumped in their seats. One after another, the bridges started reporting hounds. One was approaching the Theodore Roosevelt Memorial. Another one was coming across the Arlington Memorial. A third was coming across the Francis Scott Key. Two more were making their way across the George Mason Memorial, and a sixth was on the smaller Arland Williams Jr. Memorial.

"That's six," Amy said.

"Where do you want to start?" Brad asked.

"Francis Scott Key," Paul said.

Brad fired up the engine and sped north in the parkway to the far bridge.

The hound was standing at the line of salt when they arrived. It was growling and snapping its massive jaws at the bridge watch. When Paul and Amy got out of the car and started to approach, it looked at them with its glowing red eyes. They could feel the hate coming through that gaze.

"Well," Paul said, "we might get lucky and just have to go one at a time tonight."

Amy nodded. Focused on the hound, she started spinning her staff and moving to the left. Paul looked back to the hound and started moving to the right.

This time, Paul noted, the hound ignored Amy. It kept its eyes on Paul and shifted its stance as Paul approached. When Paul pulled out the sword from the sheath on his hip, it glowed so brilliantly that it flooded that end of the bridge in blue light. The blue flames leaped and licked from the blade, reaching toward the hound.

The hound lunged toward Paul, stopping just short of the salt, and its head stretched toward him, jaws snapping and throat roaring. In response, Paul thrust the sword at the hound. The hound flinched back a bit, then stretched toward Paul again, snapping.

The beast's fetid breath made Paul's stomach turn. Gritting his teeth, he moved closer and swung the sword across his front, preparing to strike. The hound snapped his jaws and tried to reach Paul, but the line of salt stopped him. The blade of Paul's sword nicked across its nose, leaving a trail of black blood.

The hound howled and snapped, trying to catch the sword and take it away. Paul quickly moved underneath and slashed the sword across the lower part of the hound's jaw. With a loud howl, the hound pulled back.

Paul could see Amy out of the corner of his eye. She was jumping across the salt, jabbing with the staff, smacking it across the hound's back and ribs, and jumping back, all to no effect. The hellhound just wasn't going to be distracted. It wanted Paul.

It jumped back toward Paul, trying to bite at his head. Paul leaned back and stabbed up into the hound's mouth. The blade pierced the roof of its mouth and poked out of the snout above. Paul pulled back quickly, and the blade sliced through most of the rest of the snout before coming free.

Black blood flowed freely from the hound's mouth. The beast scrabbled around in a rage, trying to reach Paul. Paul danced to the left, toward Amy, hopped across the salt, swung his sword and sliced across the hound's right leg. Then he jumped back as the hound's head swept across toward him.

Paul heard a yelp from Amy. The hound's tail had swung through and hit her, throwing her back across the salt. She lay motionless.

He yelled and attacked the hound with a fury. He jumped across the salt, stabbing and slicing, driving the hound back. The hound couldn't find purchase on the bridge slicked with its own blood and stumbled. Paul's sword opened up its neck, and as the hound fell, Paul stabbed deep into its chest. The usual mournful howl escaped it, and the brilliant blue light poured out of its eyes, mouth, and feet.

Paul pulled the sword free. As usual, it burned itself and him free of the hound's blood and bits.

He turned and ran to where Amy lay. She started to move when he got there.

"Amy," he said holding her in his arms, "are you okay?"

She opened her eyes and looked up at him.

"I forgot to duck," she said rubbing her left shoulder. "Ouch!"

He gently helped her up and she picked up her staff.

"The whole time," she said, "I was able to dash in, dash out, and avoid that stupid tail. Guess I just wasn't watching that time."

She rolled her shoulder and lifted her arm.

"Just sore," she said. "Nothing broken."

Paul smiled and they walked back to the car.

"Where next?" Brad asked.

"Arlington Memorial," Paul said, "unless something changed while we were busy."

"No changes reported," Brad said.

#

The hound at Arlington Memorial was pacing back and forth along the line of salt. When Paul and Amy got out of the car and moved toward it, it stopped and howled. Then it leapt back and forth on the road, keeping behind and clear of the salt.

Amy, again, moved to the left, and Paul moved right. The hound moved against Paul first, and Amy attacked it with the staff. It backed off from Paul's blue flame and Amy's spinning staff. Then it attacked Amy.

Paul went in on the flank and tried to make a quick end, but the hound spun and it snapped its jaws at him. Paul was caught now on the other side of the salt line. Paul sliced and swung the sword at the hound, nicking and hitting it and causing the black blood to flow, but he couldn't make a killing thrust. The hound kept coming at him.

Amy kept up her attack with the staff, hitting the hound's hind legs and back. Once, she cracked the staff so hard on the beast's back that Paul thought she must have broken it. She managed to avoid the lashing tail but wasn't able to distract the hound enough to give Paul an opening.

Paul was backing toward the side of the bridge as the hound attacked. He dodged and counterattacked with the sword. Finally, the hound charged, and Paul stepped aside. He brought the sword down hard, aiming for the head but hitting just behind the ears. The sword bit deep and severed the spine, and the hound collapsed.

He didn't wait, but immediately jumped and stabbed deeply behind the hound's shoulders and into the heart.

After the sword burned off the blood and bits, Paul stood looking around. He was on the sidewalk of Arlington Memorial Bridge. The hound had almost managed to drive him against the railing.

"Okay," he said to himself aloud. "Stay near the salt line from now on."

He joined Amy and walked back to the car.

"The hounds at the other bridges left," Brad said.

"That leaves four that we know of," Amy said.

"Well, it's a good thing they left," Paul said, still breathing heavily. "I'm done for the night."

A freshening breeze blew from the west. Paul closed his eyes and took a deep breath. The air didn't have the taint of the hounds or the city; it felt good to breathe it. When at last he opened his eyes, he stood for a moment, staring up at the sky.

"Where are the stars?" he asked.

Everyone else looked up.

"Clouds must have rolled in," Brad said.

Paul sniffed the air again.

"Smells like rain," Paul said. Then he saw a flash in the distance. "And lightning. We're going to have a storm."

"Oh, no!" Amy said. "The rain will wash away the salt!"

Brad immediately got on the radio.

"Bring in all bridge watches," he said. "Get everyone back to the hotel. Over." He changed channels on the radio and contacted the sites to warn them.

"Yeah, with the salt gone, we have only one place to defend," Paul said.

They climbed into the Crossover, bringing the team from the Arlington Memorial watch with them, and headed back to the hotel. Just as they were pulling in, raindrops started to splatter on the windshield. Other watch teams pulled in behind them and they got into the hotel.

"Get salt poured across all the doorways," Brad told people. "Make sure it's in a spot where it won't get washed away."

Bags and rounds of salt disappeared from the stash near the main entrance as people did their best to make salt lines across doors and ground floor window sills.

The storm blew in with a gust of wind that whipped the trees around, followed by pouring rain. Elder Franklin assigned people to monitor the sale lines to make sure none got washed or blown away.

Paul and Amy curled up in blankets in the lobby to sleep. If hounds arrived, they would be called to fight. The constant crashing of thunder and flashes of lighting made it difficult to sleep. Paul watched the writhing tree shadows on the wall and prayed.

TWENTY-TWO

Battle Plans

Paul breathed the cool morning air. It smelled cleaner than ever with the taint from the city washed away for a time by last night's storm. Though everyone on the mission team had reason to worry, he noticed they greeted the day and each other with smiles.

Clouds, still heavy with rain, hung in the sky, promising to wash away any effort to contain hounds at the bridges.

After breakfast, Elder Franklin called everyone into the large conference room.

"We cannot wait here for the hounds," he said. "We cannot risk the sites and the work we've done. We must be aggressive and strike now. We've organized four rifle squads, led by our veteran members. Today, those of you in those squads will drill in the play fields across the road. We don't have the luxury of time to provide complete training, but we will do our best.

"This afternoon, we will move those squads, our pastors, Paul and Amy, and myself to Foggy Bottom. We know many of the hounds have been coming out of the metro tunnels from there. We have, we think, four hounds left to fight, as well as an unknown number of other enemies.

"But fight we must and we must fight today." Elder Franklin lowered his grey head a moment, then raised it to continue.

"We will assign some people to bring pastors back from the sites after we break up from here. Others will need to break out the rest of the rifles and weapons from the storage racks. Ammunition will need to be sorted and magazines loaded. We have a lot of work to do.

"Let us pray."

The elder stood in silent prayer for a few minutes, then led the group in the Lord's Prayer.

After the "Amen," everyone went to their tasks.

"Paul, Amy," the elder said as they passed him, "I would like you two to work with the squads today. It will be critically important that you all react to the hounds and other enemies without getting in each other's way. Understood?"

"Absolutely," Paul said.

"Yes," Amy said.

Out on the play fields, Brad directed the rifle squads in some basic movement drills and practiced signals and reactions. Then he added Paul and Amy to the drills. All the while, rain sprinkled, misted, and fell in random showers.

"Keep in mind," he said during a pause, "we'll be in a confined area and the most firepower we have is in the squads. The pastors, the elder, and Paul and Amy will be almost completely defenseless. We need to keep those people in the center of our operation."

He had laid out some traffic cones to represent a metro tunnel and arrayed the squads, two on each side of the tunnel. Paul and Amy were in the middle. The two lead squads formed two arrows pointing in the direction of travel.

"The front squads must be prepared to fire on anything but hounds that appear in front of us. The squads in the back provide coverage on the flanks and rear. We don't know what that demon may have waiting, but if it is affected by bullets, we'll give them plenty," Brad said wiping rain from his face. "When hounds appear, our response is to open the front for Paul and Amy, since our firepower has no effect on the hounds. Paul and Amy move forward and deal with the hounds. If the fight forces them back, the squads fall back, keeping the pastors and the elder behind and protected.

"If the fight moves ahead, the squads maintain about a ten-meter separation. Give them room to work, hold your fire, and be prepared to sweep ahead once the hound or hounds are dispatched.

"We're going to practice this until we have it down."

Brad started the formation at one end of the cones and had the rifle squads move slowly forward. Paul and Amy stayed in the middle of the formation. Then Brad shouted, "Hounds!" The front squads moved aside and Paul and Amy jumped to the front. Brad shouted, "Back!" Paul and Amy pretended the hounds were driving them back and the squad formations shuffled back, maintaining their relative positions.

At the signal, "Forward!" Paul and Amy swept forward and the squads moved up. Brad called out, "Hounds down!" The squads moved up, enveloping around Paul and Amy, and the formation continued down the pretend tunnel.

"Pretty good," Brad said. "Could be a bit crisper." He pointed to some people in one of the rear squads. "You must maintain your relative position. If you are out of position and we start shooting things in the tunnels, you'll either be shooting squad mates or they'll be shooting you."

Brad ran them through the routine several more times, even though the rain was soaking everyone. It wasn't cold, and after a while most were able to ignore the wet.

"The rain is a distraction," Brad told Paul when he broke up the training and everyone was heading back to the hotel for lunch and change into dry clothes. "That's a good thing. If they can respond to the signals and maintain their discipline when they're wet, uncomfortable, and being rained on, the tunnels won't be a problem."

"I thought you were just a sadist," Paul said, smiling.

"Well, that, too," Brad said. Then he looked at Amy. "Those little vaults into the front were a nice added touch. A bit showy, though."

He grinned and Amy blushed.

"I was getting bored," she said.

"Too bad I didn't have a real hound to throw at you," Brad said with a laugh.

#

Paul trudged upstairs to his family's rooms. He was tired, soaked to the skin, and ready for a shower. Mom came across the main room and wrapped him in her arms. Paul hugged her back, but she held him tight for a few moments longer.

"Oh, Paul," she said. "I've been worried and scared for you. We heard all the stories and reports of what happened. All we could do was pray and hope God protected you." Then she backed off, wiping the wet off her arms, and said, "You're soaked!"

"We've been practicing in the park across the street," Paul said. "We're going into the tunnels later today to finish this thing off."

Mom looked at him. Paul saw the concern and love in her eyes. So much had changed in the last year, especially in the last few weeks. He smiled at her.

"I want a shower," Paul said. "Then I'm going to get into some fresh clothes and join the squads."

Tears formed in Mom's eyes. Paul knew she was afraid.

"Don't worry, Mom," he said. "We'll be well protected. And you know God is with us."

She nodded, but a tear escaped and trailed down her cheek.

"I know," she said. "But, you're my son. I can cry and fret if I want to." She sniffed, then waved her hand in front of her face. "And, yes, you do need to shower and change. You're getting pretty ripe."

#

Paul toweled his hair as he went back to his room. The shower felt good. It wasn't as hot as he would have liked, but he felt clean again. He got into fresh clothing and strapped the sword around his waist. He made sure the Old Timer found its way into his jeans pocket.

He would leave his pack behind this time, but the staff would go with him. He put on the vest, feeling the comforting closeness of the leather around his torso. He gathered up all his dirty clothing, stuffed it in a laundry bag, and carried it out to the hall.

"The toxic cleanup is finished, Mom," he said coming back into the main room.

She smiled at him, then looked oddly at the sword on his hip.

"You look like someone from the sixteenth century," she said. "Except in jeans."

Paul laughed and went back to his room. He picked up a light windbreaker, grabbed his staff, looked around the room, and left.

"Well, I'm ready to go," he said.

Mom came up to him and took hold of his face in her hands.

"I love you, Paul," she said. "Do well and come back."

"I love you, too, Mom. I will."

She wrapped her arms around his neck and hugged him until he thought he would pass out. But he hugged her back. She let go, kissed his cheek, and patted his chest.

"See you later, Mom," Paul said and left.

#

Paul hung out in the lobby, waiting for Amy. Some people he knew went by, busy with their tasks. But when they saw Paul, they waved and smiled. He smiled and waved back. A few people his age went by, laughed, and waved. He smiled back and waved.

Everyone is very friendly, all of a sudden, he thought.

Finally, Brad came by.

"We're about ready to form up," Brad said, smiling. "We'll all meet in the conference room in ten minutes."

"Okay," Paul said.

Brad grinned and left for the conference room.

That was weird, Paul thought.

Amy came up next. She was dressed in fresh jeans and shirt, and had a fanny pack. She'd left her backpack behind but had her staff.

She smiled at him, then started laughing.

"What's so funny?"

Amy got into her little fanny pack and pulled out a tissue. She put it up to Paul's right cheek and started rubbing.

"Silly," she said. "Your mom left her mark."

Then Paul realized Mom must have had a fresh coat of lipstick when she'd kissed his cheek.

"I can't get it all, Paul," Amy said, laughing. "You'll have to go in the restroom and clean it off."

When he came back from the restroom, the lipstick mark was gone, but his cheek was red from the effort.

"Do I look okay?" he asked Amy.

"You look fine," she said. "Let's go to the conference room."

#

There were no grand speeches, just serious people getting ready for serious work. Brad oversaw the squad preparations. Squad members checked each other's equipment, weapons, and ammunition. Each person in a squad carried several magazines of ammunition, and each rifle was fitted with a high-intensity light.

Paul and Amy watched from the sidelines. Their equipment was simple. Staffs for both of them, a vest and a sword for Paul.

Amy reached into her fanny pack and pulled out the two ornate vials. She went to a sideboard with refreshments and unstoppered the vials. She filled each with fresh water and replaced the stoppers.

She then went over to Elder Franklin.

"Would you please pray over these vials?" she asked. "I have a feeling they need a blessing."

Elder Franklin prayed and blessed the vials and her.

She tucked them back into her fanny pack as she returned to Paul.

"All set," she said.

Paul knew Amy got "feelings" about things, so he didn't bother to ask what she was up to. He just nodded and they went back to watching the preparations.

Elder Franklin got up when Brad told him everyone was ready. He gave a brief prayer, then prayed silently for a moment. Then he said, "Amen."

The room chorused, "Amen."

At the front door of the hotel, two large olive-drab trucks waited, engines rumbling in the rain. Someone had found some military vehicles, and they had canvas covers over the back.

"We'll arrive dry, at least," someone said.

The squads split between the trucks. Paul, Amy, and the elder got in the first one and the pastors got in with the remaining squads in the second.

It was dry inside the back of the truck. Someone closed the tailgate and locked it. Paul heard some shouts, then the trucks rumbled away from the hotel and toward the highway.

The trucks weren't fast, but they were steady. Wind fluttered the canvas sides and came through, but the wet stayed out. They could see the other truck and some of the scenery out the open back;

otherwise, they just looked at the people sitting on the wood benches on the other side.

They went along the Potomac River on the George Washington Parkway, then across on the Arlington Memorial Bridge. After swinging around the Lincoln Memorial, they went straight north on Twenty-Third Street to Washington Circle.

Rain spattered the trucks all the way into the city, then stopped. When they started climbing out of the trucks, the streets around Washington Circle were shiny with wet.

The trucks had pulled up at the First Street NW intersection, next to the plaza that was the Metro station for Foggy Bottom and George Washington University. Even after the rains of the last two days, the multitude of hellhound tracks and trails were visible leading in and out of the station.

Brad got the squads in formation and gathered the rest of the team into the center.

"Move out!" he shouted.

The formation moved to the subway entrance and they started down the stairs. The squad rifles swept across the fronts, sides, and rear of the formation as it moved.

TWENTY-THREE

Darkness

"LIGHTS!" Brad ordered. Everyone turned on the flashlights attached to the rifles. Light beams knifed across the front and sides of the of the passageway as the rifles swept their zones. The lead squads kept a steady pace and followed the trails left by the hellhounds into the depths of the subway.

Paul and Amy led the elder and pastors, but that just meant they walked ahead of them. Everyone kept their heads swiveling and looking, not wanting to be surprised by anything.

The ambient light became dimmer and the flashlights seemed to grow brighter as they descended to the platform. There were hellhound footprints here, lots of them, burned into the concrete of the stairs and boarding area. The trails led down to the subway tracks and turned east, toward Union Station.

None of the prints left by the hounds still glowed, but the sulfurous smell still hung in the air, along with the smell from survivors also drifted in the air here. Amy patted her fanny pack after the group scrambled and climbed off the platform and reformed on the tracks.

"I have two of the mentholated cream masks here," she said. "They were passing them around to the squads before we left and I grabbed a couple. It'll probably get bad as we get closer."

Paul nodded and smiled. Amy thought of everything. He loosened the sword in the sheath. The hilt felt warm to his touch. He looked down and there was a faint blue glow coming from the blade.

"We're on the right path," he said. "The blade is starting to glow. I don't know if that means we're close, or it's just reacting to the environment."

"Should you get it out?" Amy asked.

"I don't think so," he said. "Not yet."

As they moved forward, under Brad's direction, Paul kept his hand on the hilt.

Paul knew from studying the maps of the Metro that it was about three miles from the Foggy Bottom station to Union Station. Somewhere along that tunnel, the demon must have set up his command center. Information from some of the recon teams early in the mission had reported hound activity near the McPherson Square station. After that point, the tunnel turned southeast toward Gallery Place-Chinatown and Judiciary Square stations. This leg would be about a mile in the dark.

The tunnel grew darker, and the flashlights became the primary light source. The beams from the rifle-mounted lights flashed and sliced across the tunnel as the rifles swept across the tunnel and tracks.

The lead squads kept slow, a steady walk, sweeping lights across side passages and openings into the tunnel. The two squads in the back kept watch over the flanks and rear.

Brad called a break after they'd gone about an eighth of a mile into the tunnel. Half the squad members sat and relaxed; the others kept an alert watch. After five minutes, they switched. Some grabbed a snack, or drank from bottles while resting. When Brad ordered the squads to move out, everyone was back up and alert.

A dim ruddy glow came from far down the tunnel when they were about a quarter mile in. Paul saw it first, and whispered to Brad.

"Hounds ahead," he said.

Paul's sword was glowing furiously in its sheath, but he left it there.

Brad didn't say anything until the glow was more pronounced and the dark shape of the hound could be seen.

"Hounds!" he shouted.

Paul drew the sword. He and Amy jumped ahead of the rifle squads as the front two squads collapsed against the sides of the tunnel. Once Paul and Amy were past, the squads reformed behind them.

The glow from the sword bathed the front of the tunnel in blue, contrasting with the ruddy glow from the hound approaching them. Amy moved to the left and Paul shifted to the right.

Sulfurous smells wafted down the tunnel as the hound's tracks burned and scorched into the concrete and iron of the rails. The hound kept coming down the center of the tunnel.

"Watch the tracks," Paul said to Amy. He knew they could trip or break an ankle with those iron rails underfoot.

"Yeah," Amy said. She started her staff spinning and danced ahead a bit.

Paul swung the sword in an arc across his front and the blue flame licked out toward the hound. The hound growled, snapped its jaws, leaped to close the distance between itself and Paul and Amy. Paul then realized there was no line of salt to prevent the hound from attacking.

Amy feinted against the right side of the hound's head and Paul lashed at its left side with flame from the sword. It tried to step back and threw its head up, and Paul swung and sliced into its left shoulder.

The pain from the slice drew a howl and a counterattack, with the hound trying to bite down on Paul's head. Paul dodged the hound's attack and danced back, avoiding the rails. In the process, he left a slice on the hound's nose.

Amy dodged a sweep of the tail and made a spinning strike at it that landed with a loud crack. The hound cried out in pain, and the last third of the tail hung limply.

Then the hound spun at Amy, who danced away and vaulted clear. That exposed its flank to Paul, who dashed in and stabbed the sword deeply into the hound's chest behind the right shoulder, piercing the heart. Blue light shot from the hound's mouth, eyes, and feet. The mournful howl echoed down the tunnel.

Paul and Amy stood a moment over the dead hound and looked down the tunnel. No other ruddy glow showed yet. Paul sheathed his sword and they walked back into the formation.

"If they didn't know we were coming before," Paul said to Brad, "they do now. We think there were four hounds left. If so, that leaves three. Chances are we'll see them all together next."

"I wish there were more of those blades," Brad said.

"Sometimes I do, too," Paul said. "But we work with the tools God gave us."

They moved past the dead hound and continued for another quarter mile before Brad called a break again. This time, everyone ate a light, cold meal in shifts with some time to rest. Paul and Amy sat in the middle of the tunnel, back to back, resting on each other, while they ate.

"Smooth move, breaking that hound's tail," Paul said.

"I just wanted to knock it away," Amy said. "I didn't think I could break it."

"Left me a nice opening." Paul could feel the muscles of Amy's back roll and flex as she moved her arms up and down from her lunch sack to her mouth. He pulled his knees up and wrapped his arms around them.

"Those hounds are more vulnerable than you might think," she said. "I think I did crack a rib or two on one of the bridge fights. And when we hit them, they get hurt and howl."

Paul looked at the tunnel behind them. Guessing, by the width of the tunnel and the size of the adult hounds, he figured two might work side by side.

Paul and Amy finished their lunches, then got up and stretched. Paul could feel the eyes of the squads on them. He was getting used to witnesses watching him and Amy after fighting one of the hounds. Was it curiosity, or fear?

Brad rallied the troops. As everyone got into formation, Paul looked down the tunnel. A dim, ruddy glow flickered far ahead.

"Brad," he said, "we have hounds. More than one, I think."

Brad shouted the command, and the front squads collapsed against the sides of the tunnel. Paul and Amy ran forward again, prepared for what would come. As the squads reformed behind them, Paul moved forward slowly, watching the ruddy glow increase and trying to see how many hounds were coming.

"There are two of them," he told Amy.

The hounds continued to approach, huge and menacing, filling the tunnel with their combined bulk and the glow they gave off. They saw Paul and Amy

Paul had never seen hellhounds in an all-out run before. They were a terrifying sight, big and fast, with their heads shaking and jaws snapping. Growls rose from their throats and echoed off the runnel walls.

Amy moved to the center and leaped high, staff spinning. She whacked each hound on the head in quick succession, then bounced into a vault back. Both hounds tried to grab her in their jaws, but smacked their heads together instead.

Paul sliced through the neck of the hound on the right, bathing it in blue flame. Its black blood spurted and flowed out, covering Paul from head to foot. He rolled, dodging that hound's counter of snapping jaws, and swung heavily at the second hound, severing its left paw.

Amy spun back into the fray, pelting the left hound about the head and shoulders with multiple bone-jarring whacks. Paul rolled back and up to swipe the sword against the lower jaw of the first hound. That lower jaw hung from the hound's head for a moment, then fell to the ground.

Paul didn't have time to think of what was happening; he just reacted. He dove under the front feet and thrust up into the chest, killing the first hound. Blue light filled the tunnel as the first hound died.

Paul moved quickly to attacked the hound on the left. He slashed down across the left shoulder of the second hound, eliciting a tremendous howl. Paul gathered his remaining strength as Amy continued to batter the hound that was now collapsed to the floor. From the corner of his eye, Paul saw a third hound coming down the tunnel.

Paul jumped high and came down, thrusting the sword deep into the chest of the second hound. It died in a furious blast of blue flame and light, and Paul and Amy turned to face the third hound. Paul's legs felt rubbery, he was breathing hard, and the sword was feeling heavy in his hand. Still he stood tall to face the next challenge.

The third hound charged them at a full run, growling ferociously and snapping and swinging its head in fury. Paul and Amy moved to the center of the tunnel as if to face the charge directly.

The hound leaped at last, straight for where Paul and Amy stood. Amy vaulted to the left and Paul dodged right. Amy's staff battered across the sides and back of the hound as it passed. Paul's sword bathed the hound in blue flame as he swung it hard and sliced the hound open from shoulder to hip.

The hound hit the ground, entrails spilling out on the rails and concrete. It spun at Paul, and bit down on his right shoulder.

The pain was worse than anything he'd ever experienced. It overwhelmed him in a crushing wave of darkness and despair. He fell for what seemed like a long time before finally hitting the ground. He could hear Amy shouting, but her voice seemed to be coming from far away.

He struggled to get up, but his entire body felt heavy with fatigue, and the sword was like lead in his hand. Even staying conscious was to much effort.

He pulled himself up against the side of the tunnel and forced his eyes open.

The hound lay on the ground, its head flailing, trying to reach Paul again. Lying in a pool of entrails was the hounds heart, still beating and glowing red. Paul stumbled forward, lifted the sword and hacked clumsily at the heart.

The hound died in a burst of flaming blue light just as Amy reached Paul and touched him. The sword glowed blue and burned off the blood and bits from Paul and Amy. Then it winked out. Paul looked at it for a minute, sheathed it, took a step, and fell into darkness.

Somewhere in the darkness, he could hear screaming.

TWENTY-FOUR

Healing

I AM with you always, a voice said to him out of the darkness. *Consider the birds of the air and the lilies of the field. They neither sow nor reap. Yet I care for them. Think how much more I value you than them.*

"He bit me, Father," he said to the darkness. "I'm dying. He'll drag me to hell!"

No, my son, it is just a small hurt. You are mine and will stay mine. Nothing can take you away from my love and that is certain.

"It's dark, Father."

You will go back to the light soon. When you do, you will complete your task.

Paul felt a comfort from the darkness. Then he heard voices, indistinct at first, but clearing and getting stronger.

#

"He's still with us, barely."

"So much blood!"

"That's a nasty bite and he's losing a lot of blood. I don't know …"

Paul felt a sharp, burning pain in his right shoulder. Someone was poking and prodding at his wounds. There was a pinprick in his left shoulder.

"This antibiotic might help. We didn't bring enough medical equipment for this …"

"Can you stitch the shoulder back together?"

"I don't think that is possible."

"I can't stop the bleeding!"

Someone close by held his left hand.

"He won't make it if we can't stop the bleeding!"

"I don't think there's much hope for him."

"If there is another hound, we're all dead."

"Where's the sword?"

"Let me try this."

Drops of a sweet elixir entered his mouth and he greedily swallowed them. A few more drops entered, and he moved his mouth around, savoring the strangely familiar flavor and sweet healing. He took a deep breath.

"The bleeding is stopping."

More of the elixir entered his mouth. He swallowed, feeling stronger. He opened his eyes and Amy floated into his field of view. She smiled down on him.

He tried to sit up, but the pain in his shoulder stopped him.

"Ouch!" he said.

"Here," Amy said putting the vial to his lips. "Drink this."

He drank deeply, then shivered. He flashed back to the mission and when he used the healing potions.

"Where'd you get that?" His voice shook as the elixir coursed through his system and he vibrated. It was over in a moment. He opened his vest and looked at his shoulder. The wounds were healing leaving puckered scars. Paul's shirt was mostly destroyed on the right side, and bloody. He tore away the ruined part, then closed the vest.

"The Lord God provides," Amy said and hugged Paul's neck. When she let him go, she took the vial, put the stopper in place and put it back in the little pack.

Paul rolled his shoulders settling the vest in place. There was some damage to the vest and some blood stains.

Brad came over and looked at Paul, his injuries gone and he stood there with no sign of being hurt.

"You guys never cease to amaze me," he said. "You ready to move on?"

"Yeah," Paul said. "I'm good."

"Ready," Amy said, picking up her staff.

Paul looked around. There were no dead hounds nearby.

"Where are we?" he asked Amy.

"We carried you past the hounds," she said. "It was nasty and reeked, so we grabbed you and moved down the tunnel."

"Oh," he said. "How long was I out?"

"Long enough for me to panic."

"Sorry."

"It wasn't your fault; it was that nasty dog hurt you. I thought I . . . I thought we lost you."

She turned her face away from him and pretended to adjust her fanny pack.

Everyone was back in formation and Brad started them moving. Paul watched Amy for a moment as they started moving.

"Thanks for having that elixir," he said.

"I forgot all about it until I noticed your vest. These things we got during the Troubles always prove useful. This morning, the vials just had fresh water. I had Elder Franklin bless them and I put them in my little pack. What happened since then, I don't know. But when we needed them, they're full of healing elixir."

"Well, one is," Paul said. "Hope we don't need more than that."

Paul looked ahead. The tunnel was black, with the flashlights licking the walls, ceiling, and floor as the squads moved. The movement almost became boring, until at last they saw a dim light ahead.

"What's that?" Paul asked Brad.

"I think we're close to McPherson Square," he said. "That's probably the station up ahead."

McPherson Square station had just very dim light filtering down the stairways from the surface.

"It's late in the day," Brad said. He stopped the squads at the platform and sent one squad up to scout the surface. Trails of hellhound tracks led up and down the stairs, but the bulk of the scorched trails moved along the tunnel.

The scouts returned and reported seeing a few survivors in the area around McPherson Square station. The sky was still overcast, they said, and it was starting to get dark.

Brad sent another squad with instructions to go just a couple of hundred yards ahead. When they came back, they said the tunnel started curing to the southeast. Otherwise, all they saw beyond the flashlights was black.

Brad came over to Paul.

"What do you think? Are there are any more hounds?"

Paul pulled the sword from the sheath. The blade was glowing dimly.

"I can't promise there aren't any," he said. "The blade's glowing, but it might not be hounds. Or if there are hounds, they may not be very close. For all we know, there are still some around Union Station."

"Well, I guess we just stay prepared for anything, then," Brad said.

Paul shrugged and nodded. "I have a feeling the squads will be doing a bit more in this next phase."

Brad got everyone formed up again and started them moving. More than a few cast a last look at the dimming light of the station as they moved into the pitch dark of the tunnel.

The tunnel began to take a long, sweeping curve to the southeast. The rifle-mounted flashlights continued knifing across the walls, ceilings, and floor as the squads moved slowly along.

Suddenly, someone in the lead squad shouted out. A figure stood near an open access doorway on the left side of the tunnel. Ten flashlights focused on it.

Paul thought it looked like a survivor, but wasn't as thin or emaciated, and its clothing was dingy. Of course, that could have been the effect of the flashlights. It had a slack jaw, protruding cheekbones, and hollow eyes.

Paul pulled out his sword. It glowed brightly, covering the survivor with strange hues.

The survivor raised one of its hands and pointed toward the squad. It let out a shrill, bloodcurdling scream and started charging at the squads. The scream must have startled one of the squad members, because a shot rang out, then a lot of shots rang out. The sound of the shooting filled and echoed through the tunnel—nearly deafened Paul and Amy. They held their hands over their ears.

The bullets plastered the survivor against the side of the tunnel. It slid down the wall, leaving a bloody smear, and ended in a rumpled heap.

"Let's keep a firm control on our trigger fingers, people," Brad shouted when he got the firing stopped. "We have limited ammunition. We need a three-sixty-degree perimeter here. They know we're coming."

Brad handed Paul and Amy two small packages.

"Ear plugs," he said. "You'll need them."

Paul and Amy opened the packages and inserted the soft, foam plugs in their ears. Brad distributed ear plugs to the elder and the pastors. The squad leaders passed ear plugs to their squads.

The formation started moving again. They hadn't gone more than ten steps when a wall of people came into view. Like the one just down the tunnel, these were hollow-eyed and slack-jawed and shuffled toward the squads. As soon as the light touched them, they started running, hands outstretched, ready for a stranglehold.

"Line!" Brad shouted. Moving quickly, the front two squads made a ten-person firing line across their front. The other two squads kept watch over the flank and rear in a semi-circle.

"Fire!" Brad said.

The front squads opened fire, mowing down the line, but there were more ranks behind the first. The ones from behind ran over the fallen and kept coming, and some of the fallen continued to crawl forward.

"Three-round bursts," Brad shouted. "Fire!"

The line clicked a fire selector on their rifles, then opened fire again. This time, almost twice as many fell, but more kept coming from behind. Even so, a number of the fallen were still moving and crawling forward.

Paul drew his sword and pointed it at the rushing crowd. The sword blazed a brilliant blue. Flames poured out of the blade, bathing the approaching crowd until they all looked as if they were on fire.

"In the name of Jesus Christ, begone!" he yelled.

The air buffeted everyone like it was driven by an explosion. The crowd stopped moving and stood dumbstruck.

"Cease fire," Brad shouted, unnecessarily. No one had fired a shot once Paul's sword started pouring forth flames.

"They're possessed," Paul said. "Or, they were. The demon may still have a hold on them."

"They looked just like zombies," Brad said. "Fast zombies."

He looked down on the fallen. All of them had stopped moving now.

"Do you think they're clear now?" Amy asked. "Or are they like William? It took a while to get him completely clear."

"Better safe than sorry," said Paul. "Don't touch them, don't let them near you and don't leave them behind us."

"Drive them ahead?" Brad asked.

Paul nodded. "Nelchael can re-possess them, I think. William said something like that, that he could take William back."

A rotten, putrid stink came from the crowd of possessed. Squad members were already putting on their masks stacked with mentholated cream, Paul put his on, too.

Then Elder Franklin stood behind the front squads with the pastors and he held up his Bible.

TWENTY-FIVE

Last Hellhound

"I THINK WE can drive them," he said. Already, the possessed were drawing back. The pastors recited the Lord's Prayer and slowly started walking along with the elder. Before them, the possessed made a shambling retreat down the tunnel.

The elder and pastors moved slowly down the tunnel as it curved, praying and driving the possessed ahead of them. When the possessed faltered or slowed, Paul drew the sword and let the blue flame blaze out and add to the prayers.

When the tunnel straightened out, suddenly the crowd of possessed stopped, then began shuffling back to the elder and pastors. Paul leapt forward, sword drawn, and rebuked the demon possessing the survivors. They stopped, then they surged again. Paul cried out his rebuke again, the sword shining and bathing the crowd with blue flames.

Again, the possessed stopped. The elder stood with the Bible raised and the pastors holding up hands, repeating the Lord's Prayer. The possessed turned away and started a slow shuffle down the tunnel.

When the sword dimmed, the squads' flashlights played across the possessed past the nearer ranks, and Paul realized what had happened.

"Brad," he said, "we came to another group of possessed. That's what turned them back to us. We must be getting close to the demon."

"The next station is the Gallery Place-Chinatown," Brad said. "It's not far now. After that is Judiciary Square."

"Call a halt," Paul said, "and have everyone turn off their lights."

Brad complied and Paul sheathed his sword. It was pitch black, but past the possessed there was a dim ruddy glow.

"Have them turn their flashlights back on," Paul said.

The lights flicked on. The possessed were stopped again. The elder still held his Bible up, and the pastors continued to recite the Lord's Prayer, but the possessed stood where they were. A moan started from further down the tunnel, and Paul guessed there were more possessed coming their way.

He drew the sword again and went forward. The blue light shone intensely, flames leapt from the blade at the possessed. Paul cried out his rebuke once again and blue flames filled the tunnel, washing over the possessed. They fell back, driven by the pressure of the flames. Paul shouted the rebuke again.

"In the name of Jesus Christ, begone!"

Again, the tunnel filled with blue flames and the possessed drew back. This time, though, when Paul came back to the squad line, he stumbled and had trouble sheathing the sword. Amy grabbed his left arm and put it around her neck.

"I'm spent for a bit," he said. "That takes some out of me. I need to rest. I have a feeling we'll need this for the demon, too."

They made headway down the tunnel for about a hundred yards, and the possessed slowed and stopped again. The ruddy light behind them had grown brighter.

Elder Franklin and the pastors came back behind the squad line.

"We're having no effect," the elder said. "We keep praying and they just stand there. But, they aren't coming back this way yet."

"I'm just glad they aren't running anymore," said Brad.

"I hate to say it," Paul said, "but we may not be able to save many, or any, of these survivors. We've weakened the demon's hold on them, but I don't know how long we can continue to go on like this. The demon will possess them again, given time."

"You're right," the elder said. "We've done what we can with these possessed."

Elder Franklin bowed his head in a silent prayer and ended with an audible "Amen."

Paul looked at the possessed. They just stood where they were, staring straight ahead at whatever was in front of them. Flashlights played across their ranks. Most were gray versions of the survivors the mission had dealt with on the surface. They were hollow-eyed and filthy, completely without motivation or direction. Then he noticed there was some movement from far in the back.

The ruddy glow grew brighter.

"I think we have another hound coming," Paul said.

The possessed were moving to the sides of the tunnel, making way for something. The reddish glow increased, tinging the possessed tinged with its eerie light.

Brad watched until the familiar dark shape of the hound came into view.

"Hound," he shouted the order. The front squads, now well-drilled in the routine, collapsed to the sides of the tunnel, and Paul and Amy moved forward. The squads closed ranks behind them.

Paul held Amy's hand until the hound broke through the possessed and faced them.

"Today," it said in a deep, booming, snarling voice, "you die."

The hound was taller and broader than any they face before.

"Not if you die first," Paul said and drew his sword. "You are a liar and the slave of liars!"

The light flowed through the sword. Paul could see it glowing through his own flesh and Amy's. Flames lashed out the tip of the blade, brighter than ever. The hound flinched as intense blue flames smashed against it. Dark spots appeared on the hound's flesh where the blue flame seared it.

Amy danced to the left, staff spinning. Paul, holding the sword straight out toward the hound, moved forward and slightly to the right. The blue flames continued to flow and burn and sear the hound.

"You are a lie!" Paul said and leapt at the hound's head.

The hound tried to grab Paul in its jaws, but Paul twisted and brought the blade down through its snout. Paul's leap carried him over to the left, with his hand still gripping the sword's hilt, and the sword still piercing the hound's snout. Just as Paul's feet touched the ground , an ugly crunch sounded, and the sword came free, splitting the hound's snout from nose to eyes.

Paul spun, swinging the now free sword and severed the left leg just below the hound's shoulder. At the same time, Paul saw Amy in mid-leap, jabbing her staff into the right eye of the hound. Howls of pain rent the air in the tunnel.

The hound lost its footing and rolled to its left. Paul jumped to the hound's right shoulder and drove the blade into its heart.

"I said," Paul shouted as blue flame shot out of the hounds eyes and feet, "not if you die first."

He pulled the sword free. Blue light burned off the blood and bits. When the blade was clean, Paul sheathed the sword and moved back toward the squad line with Amy.

The possessed started shuffling back down the tunnel.

"That," Paul said to Brad, "is the last hound."

"Good," Brad said. "Then let's move out."

The squads advanced, enveloping Paul, Amy, the elder, and the pastors, and followed the retreating possessed. The ruddy glow was still down the tunnel, but it looked more like the flickering of a campfire now. The possessed were heading straight for it and Paul guessed the final confrontation was coming.

A sulfurous smell filled the tunnel, like rotten eggs on fire. Paul looked at the elder; the elder shrugged. Paul was about to make a smart remark about fire and brimstone preaching, but decided against it.

The tunnel opened into a round cavernous room with a crowd of the possessed surrounding a huge fire that burned in the center. At one side, there was a dais with a throne-like chair and a figure sitting on it.

At the sight of the figure on the throne, Paul stopped short. He hadn't expected the demon to look like this. He'd expected some hideous creature, obviously evil. This creature looked … well, a lot like Gabriel, beautiful and wise. Paul could see why William had worshiped him. He had curly hair and wore a rich red robe. Every finger had a ring.

But even as Paul noticed all this, he saw something else, something hard, mean, and spiteful. They eyes were red, and the mouth was twisted into a cruel sneer.

The squad formation entered the room, maintaining its full perimeter security.

"Who dares enter my domain, unbidden?" the figure on the throne asked. His voice boomed in the chamber; it was deep and deadly, but beautiful in a way, like his face. "Who invades my place, kills my pets, and violates my presence?"

Paul moved to the front squads and slipped ahead of them. He approached a few steps, then stopped.

"You do not belong here," he said. "You must return to where you belong."

The demon sneered. "Who are you to tell me that I do not belong here?" He raised his right hand and gestured. Suddenly, Amy was at Paul's side and the two of them were held in place by some force. With a wave of his left hand, the squads, the pastors, and the elder were pushed back several yards.

"I come here," Paul said, struggling against the invisible bonds, "at the bidding of the Lord God. He says you do not belong here."

The demon flipped his right hand at Paul in a dismissive wave. Paul's head snapped to the side in response to an invisible slap. *That hurt!* Paul tried to move, but couldn't. He was bound to the spot. A core of panic grew. *Was this a trap?* he thought. *Was this his plan all along?*

"Anyone can claim to come at His bidding," he said. "You come as a destroyer, killing my pets!"

"You are Nelchael," Paul said, still struggling against the invisible bonds. "One of the fallen, servant of Satan, and you don't belong here."

The demon looked at Paul directly. Paul knew that knowing the demon's name was key to driving him out. He could see it on the demon's face.

"You have no authority to tell me I do not belong here! I was given this domain by Satan himself! He rules this plane and your God can't do anything about it."

"Wrong, Nelchael," Paul said, drawing on his faith and trying to surpassing his panic. "God, Jesus Christ, is Lord and Master of the

Universe. He created it. He created you, as a matter of fact, as well as Satan. Much as you don't want to accept it, you must leave when you are told to do so in His name."

A movement at his right caught Paul's eye. It was Elder Franklin standing against an invisible barrier, holding up his Bible, with the pastors behind him, praying.

"You have no authority!" Nelchael said. His voice was an angry roar, but Paul heard a note in it that reminded him of a child having a tantrum.

"Oh, we have authority," Elder Franklin said. "We have authority by the grace of Jesus Christ, as his followers. We can command you to leave in His name."

The demon looked at the elder and sneered. Then he looked at Paul and back to the elder.

"I'm here to rule this domain! No one on this plane has the power to remove me." he said. "It was given to me by Satan and I delivered thousands of souls to him for it! I plan to deliver more."

The demon pointed his be-ringed hand at Paul and Amy. "I will deliver Paul and Amy and you cannot stop me. Even though you took my pets, I have all these in my possession," he waived at the crowd of possessed people around the chamber, "and my imps. My imps are like myself, they are immortal. You cannot kill them. There is nothing you can do to stop me."

A crowd of small demons, imps, appeared from behind the throne. Paul thought they were the ugliest things he had ever seen. Oversized ears on knobby heads, straggly hair, pointed teeth in mouths that looked like slits in paper. Their arms and legs were boney with round, arthritic-looking joints. They bounced around the throne, some bowing and worshiping the demon.

Nelchael stood and looked lustfully at Amy and Paul, and Paul automatically tried to put his left arm protectively in front of Amy. He was still bound. The core of panic grew.

"Some torment before I deliver you to Satan is in order," the demon said. His eyes sparkled red. "You must pay for killing all my pets, especially the puppies. Then I'll deliver you to Satan and he'll reward me with more hounds and imps."

Paul's right hand was near his sword. He wrapped his fingers around the sword hilt. His panic grew and he sought comfort in the familiar hilt, the only thing he could reach. Then he felt the power of the Holy Spirit flow through the sword and into him. The invisible bindings came loose.

"You will deliver no more souls, if we can help it," the elder said.

Paul drew the sword.

TWENTY-SIX

Demon Battle

"WHERE DID YOU get that?" Nelchael's eyes widened when he saw the sword. "Who gave that to you?" The demon stood from his throne and the red light in the room increased beyond that thrown by the fire. Nelchael held out his left hand toward the sword. "You cannot hold that blade!"

The demon pulled his right arm up and a fireball appeared in his hand. He threw the fireball at Paul.

Paul immediately pointed the sword at the fireball and a blue flame licked out and blasted the fireball out of existence.

"As I said, Nelchael, I come here at the bidding the Lord God," Paul said. He raised the sword and the blue flames licked out of the tip of the blade, driving back the red light in the chamber. A glowing blue nimbus of light surrounded Paul, Amy, and grew toward the elder and pastors. As the nimbus grew, the invisible barrier disappeared and it wrapped around the squads as well.

A wave of imps charged at Paul and Amy, but Paul directed the sword's energy at them and they tumbled back into the throne.

"Release your hold on the people," Paul ordered Nelchael. "Release them now!" *It's worth a shot,* he thought.

"No! No!" the demon grimaced and gnashed his teeth. "You can't take them from me! They are mine! Mine!"

Like a major league baseball player, Nelchael raised his right arm again and threw a fireball at Paul. This time, Paul wasn't quite quick enough and the fireball was only deflected. It careened away from the sword's energy and smashed into a wall to Paul's left, leaving a huge burning hole.

"Let them go!" Paul said. His confidence strengthened as he felt Elder Franklin near him on the right. The nimbus expanded more and closed on the throne. Blue flames from the sword licked at the demon. Nelchael shifted back to the throne.

"No, they are mine! They will always be mine! You can't take them."

"We can. We will." Elder Franklin joined in, holding the Bible in front of him. "You must obey."

"You lie," Paul yelled at Nelchael. "You had William, but we freed him from your hold. He told us of your lies and deceit. You must obey us!"

"No!" Nelchael waved more imps toward Paul. They charged out from the throne, screaming and reaching. Blue flames from the sword dashed them back against the throne again.

Nelchael looked at his possessed. They started moving toward the squads.

"They obey me," he said. "You cannot take them and I won't release them!"

Paul could see the squads getting ready to fire on the possessed.

"Release these people, Nelchael, in the name of Jesus Christ, release them!" Paul shouted. Flames leaped from the sword and the nimbus expanded to cover the demon and the throne. Blue flames bathed the demon and he cried out, his body twisting on the throne in agony.

The possessed stopped. Nelchael, still bathed in blue flame, cried.

"Release them, Nelchael," Paul said. "In the name of Jesus Christ."

The demon writhed on the throne. Finally, he pushed himself up.

"I," Nelchael said softly, "I release you."

It was like something snapped. One moment, the possessed were standing, staring blankly. The next, they were looking around.

Brad immediately got a squad moving to herd the formerly possessed out of the cavern and up to the Chinatown station.

Nelchael, the blue flamed no longer bathing him, braced against the throne. Hate glaring from his eyes, he pointed his jeweled finger at Paul.

"My imps will feast on your flesh," he said. "They will!"

He stood and immediately started throwing fireballs at Paul. Paul swung the sword at the fireballs as quickly as he could and eliminated most of them. The few he didn't, he'd manage to deflect into other parts of the cavern. A toxic-smelling smoke started to fill the air as a result of the fireballs burning holes in the cavern walls.

Then, Nelchael sent the imps again. They swarmed toward Paul and Amy, as well as the pastors and the squads. Rifles barked at the imps, but had no effect. Paul directed the energy of the sword at the imps, and back to deflecting fireballs as best he could.

"I need help," Paul said to Elder Franklin.

Franklin waved the pastors up. They put hands on Paul and started praying. Paul could feel the Holy Spirit move through him and the sword.

With a crash, blue flame burst out of the sword and drove the imps back behind the throne and again bathed the demon. The fireballs stopped.

"Nelchael," Paul said, "Send your imps back to Satan. They must go now."

"No," the demon said through clenched teeth. He tried to wave the imps to charge again, but the blue flames increased and he fell to the foot of the throne.

"Now, Nelchael," Paul said. "Send them back to Satan now."

"No, never! They are mine!"

"Do it now," Paul said. The intensity of the blue flame in creased, the prayers of the pastors and elder continued. "Do it now, or I will."

"No, you can't! They are mine! You can't send them away!" Nelchael dragged himself to stand, his eyes flaming red and a red glow forming around him. "You have gone too far."

The imps danced and cheered as Nelchael, getting a second wind, began to form new fireballs. The fireballs formed red and crackling in both the demon's hands and the imps made rude gestures at Paul and Amy and the rest of the people inside the blue nimbus.

"The hellhounds failed and the possessed failed, but I will not. I will send you to hell!" the demon shouted.

Nelchael threw the fireballs with a renewed strength. Paul raised the sword at the balls as they arced from the demon's hands. Before they were half way, the blue flames crashed into them with a violent, deafening boom that shook the walls of the cavern. The imps tumbled down at the feet of the demon, and the shock of the fireball/blue flame collision knocked Nelchael back into the throne.

"In the Name of God's only Son, Jesus Christ, you imps must leave and return to Satan!" Paul directed the full force of the sword's blue flames against the crowd of imps. "Begone!"

The nimbus expanded to cover the imps and the blue flame drove them toward a black, swirling hole that appeared in the air. The imps screamed in fear and madness and grasped at the robe, legs, and feet of the demon, trying to escape being driven out.

"Begone!" Paul shouted.

Wailing, gnashing, and with shrill screams, the imps were swept up into a whirlwind of blue flame that tossed them into the black hole. Nelchael let out a long, keening wail as the imps disappeared and the hole snapped shut. The demon struggled to stand, using his throne for support. For the first time, Paul thought he saw fear on the demon's face.

"Prepare to leave this plane, demon!" the elder shouted. Elder Franklin turned and spoke to the pastors, encouraging them. "We need prayer and faith," he said.

"Okay, Paul," the elder said. He placed his hand on Paul's shoulder and held up his Bible. "Let's close the curtain on this show."

Paul dared not take his eyes off the demon, but could hear the prayer of the people behind him and saw the blue nimbus grow and brighten. He once again felt the power of the Holy Spirit fill him as he held Amy's hand in his left, and raised the sword high in his right.

"You are a liar and a deceiver, Nelchael," Paul said. "I know your name, Nelchael, and I know you are a fallen angel, one of Satan's followers. You betrayed your Lord God, He who created you, are damned by Him. You only await His final judgement to live for eternity, burning in the lake of fire, in complete separation from Him. In God's name and in the name of His Sone, Jesus Christ, I rebuke you!"

The blue nimbus expanded to include the throne and a torrent of blue flame shot out of the sword and knocked the demon out of his throne and to the dais. He scrambled to stand again, and tried to form a fireball in his hands, but the attempts just fizzled in the blue light of the nimbus.

"You, Nelchael, possessed humans and tortured them, forcing them to do your bidding," Paul said. "You fed those you possessed to the hellhounds, taking their souls without mercy. You can receive no grace and deserve the judgement God will give you. In the glorious name of the Living God and in the name of His Son, Jesus Christ, I rebuke you!"

Again, the sword blasted out a gout of blue flame that engulfed and burned the body of the demon. He collapsed at the foot of his throne, breathing heavily. His curly hair now burnt off, and only scarred patches of scalp remained. His red robe was now just a few fluttering scraps and smoldering scars covered his body, which was taking on the wasted, starved look of a survivor.

"You are cruel, unforgiving and merciless, Nelchael," Paul said. "Your sin, like Satan's, is pride and selfishness. But, it is not for me to judge you. My task is to rebuke you and remove you from this plane. So, in the name of my Loving God, and in His Son's Name, Jesus Christ, I rebuke you!"

Nelchael didn't try to stand any more. Burns and scars covered his emaciated body and the red light in his eyes was dimmed.

"Mercy! Mercy!" he cried.

Nelchael struggled, bracing against the throne. He finally stood.

"I can't grant you mercy," Paul said. He watched the demon, who seemed to be gathering his last strength. Paul let go of Amy and reached into his pocket with his left hand. The Old Timer was there. He pulled it out and wrapped his hand around it, holding it up. "Only God can grant you mercy. It is not my place to judge you, and I do not. I name your sins, but God, in His infinite wisdom, will judge you."

Nelchael looked at Paul's left hand. He couldn't see the simple, small, Old Timer clutched in Paul's fingers. He had no idea the value of the object, or the faith of those who once owned it. It was just a simple pocket knife passed on from father to son for several generations, then given as a gift to Paul when he needed it during the Troubles. Paul saw Nelchael's distraction with his left hand.

Thanks, Sal, Paul thought. *I bet you had no idea how this simple tool could be used.*

The demon raised his own hands, again attempting to form a fireball.

"Nelchael, you must leave this plane, now!" Paul said. "In the name of God, and his Son, Jesus Christ, leave this plane!"

Blue flame again bathed the demon and his fireball attempts failed. He writhed in agony on the dais—howling, now, in his anguish—but staring at Paul's left hand.

The power of the Holy Spirit roared through the pastors, the elder, Paul, and the sword and slammed into the demon. The demon still transfixed on Paul's left hand.

"Begone!" Paul shouted.

Blue flame consumed the demon and winked out. The echo of the demon's wails bounced around the cavern for a few moments and faded.

The demon was gone and the throne and dais started to crumble.

"We have to get out of here," Paul said.

Crackling and cracking sounds came from the stone of the cavern. Rocks started falling from the ceiling.

"To the Chinatown station," Brad shouted. "Run!"

After all the precision formation since they entered the tunnels, Paul thought it was odd to see the squads break and run with the elder and pastors close behind.

Crashing and rumbling followed them to the southeast tunnel exit from the cavern. Paul and Amy climbed up on the platform and paused to look back. The walls and ceiling had collapsed on the site where the throne and huge fire were, pushing dust and debris toward them in a dense wave. Pushing Amy ahead, Paul ran to the stairs and the dim light ahead.

TWENTY-SEVEN
New Beginnings

THE GALLERY PLACE-Chinatown metro station had a dim light filtering down through the stairs from above. The squads climbed slowly, still alert to possible attacks.

Paul and Amy held hands and climbed up toward the increasing light.

"Are we done?" Amy asked.

"I think so," Paul said. The sword swung in the sheath as he moved up the stairway. "I hope so."

Elder Franklin climbed the stairs not far away, with the tight group of pastors near him. He looked over at Paul with a smile. Paul smiled and nodded in return.

They came out of the stairway into an early dawning day and walked out to a small plaza. The sky was clear and deep blue.

Brad was already on his hand-held radio, letting the trucks know where they were.

Paul and Amy moved to sit on a bench across the plaza, when Paul was distracted by a stranger walking up to them. No, there were three strangers. Then Paul recognized one of them. They all had beautiful faces and flowing hair, but their clothing shifted constantly and, by habit, Paul avoided looking at the clothes.

"Gabriel," Paul said. "What are you doing here?"

"I am just a messenger," Gabriel said. "I serve The Lord God, the Almighty, the Alpha, and the Omega."

"I know that," Paul said. "It's good to see you again."

"It is good to see you again, Paul. And you, Amy."

"What is the message?" Paul asked.

"We have come to collect some things."

"What things?" Amy asked. "The imps and demon are gone, and the hellhounds too."

"I know, my dear Amy." Gabriel indicated the angel to his right. "This is Malachi. He is another messenger of God. He is here to collect the vials you were given."

"My vials?" Amy said. She dug into her fanny pack and pulled out the two ornate crystal vials. One was empty, the other held a glowing red elixir. "Oh, these are so precious." She held them out to Malachi.

"Yes, they are," Malachi said, taking them. "They were given in mercy to help you when you most needed it. But it is time to give them back now."

Amy took one last look at the ornate crystal vials, then held them out to Malachi. "Thank you. We're grateful for the help."

Malachi touched Amy's forehead with his hand and she visibly shivered.

"We thank you, Amy," Malachi said.

Gabriel indicated the angel on his left.

"This is Michael," Gabriel said. "He is . . ."

"God's warrior-prince," Paul finished. He now realized where the sword came from and why it had such power. "I expect you have come for the sword, Michael." Paul unbuckled the sword, rolled up the belt around the sheath, and held it out to Michael.

"Yes, Paul," Michael said. "I have come for the sword. We are pleased that you used it well." Michael took the sword.

Faith in God, Paul thought, *that was all the weapon we really needed. The sword was just an instrument to help drive home the will of God.*

"One more thing, Paul," Gabriel said. "I need to collect the vest."

"The vest?" Paul said. Much as he'd bonded with the sword and did not want to give it up, the vest seemed like a part of him. He slowly unbuttoned it and slid it off his shoulders.

"I hope I didn't get it all messed up," he said, handing it to Gabriel. "I'm going to really miss that vest."

"I know," Gabriel said. "But this vest is no more than the armor of God. You will always have the armor of God, Paul, and you do not need this vest for that."

"So, Gabriel, is this your item?"

"It is the item for which I am responsible, yes."

"Thank you, then. It kept me alive."

"I know, Paul, and you are welcome. Know that God loves you and you are precious to him." Gabriel turned to Amy. "Know that God loves you and you are precious to him."

Michael stepped forward and put his hand on Paul's shoulder.

"You are a good warrior for God," he said. As he spoke, Paul felt a cleansing warmth clear the fatigue and hunger from his body.

"We must go now," Gabriel said. "Your work here isn't done. There are a lot of souls here who need your help being brought into God's love."

Then they were alone. Paul looked at Amy. Her face was streaked with tears.

"Are you okay?" Paul asked, taking her hand.

"Oh, yes," she said. "I'm better than okay. I'm just full of joy. Malachi's touch made me feel so alive. I don't even feel tired or hungry anymore. All I feel is God's love, more directly and powerfully than ever before in my life."

"That's pretty much how I feel," Paul said, then smiled. "I'm just not crying about it."

Amy punched his shoulder.

#

Before long, the trucks arrived to take them back to the hotel. The trip took them down to Constitution Avenue, then west to the Arlington Memorial Bridge. Paul and Amy watched out the open back of the truck as they went.

"Look," Paul said, pointing to a survivor on Constitution Avenue. "He's just sitting there."

Sure enough, the survivor just sat on the curb next to the trail he'd made during his possession. He still looked starved and emaciated, but didn't have that vacant look anymore.

They watched for others as they rode. All the other survivors they passed were sitting near their trails, too.

"They just look like they are waiting," Amy said.

"Waiting for us," Paul said. "Not just you and I, but for the whole mission team to come help them."

"I think I'll be glad to get back to that part of the mission," Amy said. "Still, I learned a few things about the bo. I'll have some new moves to show my sensei when I get home."

"I don't think he'll want you to bring a hellhound to the dojo so you can show him," Paul said.

Elder Franklin was sitting across from them in the truck bed. "Well, my best advice to you, Paul," he said, "is to never make that young lady angry."

Amy shook her staff at Paul in a mock threat.

"Good advice, Elder," Amy said.

#

At the hotel, Elder Franklin reorganized the mission back to the original tasks and Paul and Amy rode with Brad and Janet out to the high school to check on the site and the people there.

"We got a bunch of folks show up this morning," Gary said. "They said they came from the metro tunnels. How they found their way here, I have no idea, but here they are. We're doing our best to get them cleaned up, dressed, and fed."

"Those people were like William," Paul said. "They were held down in the tunnels to help protect the demon. But that all fell apart."

"Another thing about this new batch of survivors," Gary said. "Once you get them cleaned up and fed, you can touch them. And they talk to you. Even the survivors we brought in from around town can communicate now. The new survivors are still in miserable shape, and it'll take a while to get them healthy and fully functional. But this is incredible."

"It sure is," Brad said.

Just then a truck pulled up with ten survivors in it. The driver got out, dropped the gate and stairs and stood back. The survivors all stood and got out of the truck on their own and walked to the tents.

The driver saw them looking.

"Hey, we don't even need a gathering crew anymore," the driver said. "We pull up, open the back and they climb in. Just like they were waiting for us. Much more efficient!"

"So," Gary said, "rather than gather, we could use your help feeding, clothing, and doing some evangelism."

"That sounds like more fun," Amy said.

#

Paul and Amy lay on a blanket in the sand on a beach on the North Carolina Outer Banks, soaking up some late morning sun. Summer was ending. Paul was half dozing and Amy was reading. The mission had been a success, and Washington, D.C. was slowly coming back to life. The government was doing what it could to help and was making plans to return to the historic city in the future.

Complete recovery would take some time, though. Years, probably. The long absence of people had left a lot of damage unrepaired. The entire social, political, and economic infrastructure had to be rebuilt for the city to become viable again.

The survivors, though, were strong and healthy and were reclaiming their city building by building, house by house. After the mission returned home, the Shannons and Grossmans came out to the Outer Banks for a couple of weeks of rest before the weather changed, fall came on, and school started.

"We're almost sixteen now," Amy said suddenly.

"Huh?" Paul grunted, coming out of a near sleep state.

"I said, we're going to be sixteen soon."

Paul opened his eyes and saw that Amy was now sitting up. She'd set her book aside with a bookmark to hold her place.

"And?" Paul said.

"Well, I think it's long past time for you and me to start thinking about going out. Actually dating."

Paul was wide awake now. "Huh?"

"Well, we'll start school again soon, and I just don't see you surviving if you try dating some other girl."

"Dating?"

"Yes. I expect you to date me now. No more of this assuming I will go with you wherever you go, answer whenever you call, all that.

You will set a time, date, and activity and then ask me to go with you. I will reserve the right to decline."

"Decline?"

"Of course, if I decline, you will not ask another girl out. You'll just stay home."

"Why would I ask another girl to go out?"

"That's a good question. Why would you? Especially considering your very life may hang in the balance."

She bent over, throwing her shadow across his face.

"I'm serious, Mr. Shannon."

She kissed him.

<<< The End >>>

This is the second book in the Spirit Missions trilogy.

Sudden Mission by Guy L. Pace, the first book.

Satan, once one of God's favorites, now His Adversary, grows impatient with the plan and begins to harvest souls. In a fell swoop, he throws reality out of whack and the world into chaos. God calls on Paul and his friends Amy and Joe to set things right. The young teens journey through a messed up world—with a little help from an angel—struggling against everything the Adversary can throw in their path to accomplish their Sudden Mission.

With their world and their parents' lives hanging in the balance–and the Adversary sending everything from zombies to killer aliens to stand in their way–Paul will discover if he has the strength and faith to set things right again and stop Satan's harvest.

Carolina Dawn by Guy L. Pace, the last book.

Amy Grossman must decide about Paul Shannon's proposal. Guilt over Joe Banes' death still eats at her. Then there is Lucy--a competitor for Paul's affection--to deal with. She also fills her days with gardening, handling power outages, and perimeter guard duty.

A stranger arrives with dire news turning Amy's life new directions. With its very survival on the line, the community must pull together one more time.

MORE GREAT READS

***Freedom's Secret* by Amy McCoy Dees** (YA Historical Christian Fiction) Keegan O'Malley has long since escaped the Jamaican sugar plantation and found freedom in St. Augustine, Florida. He vows to find his brother and childhood friend, his journey leading him through secret tunnels, over rushing rivers, and inside smelly, pirate-filled taverns.

***The Chronicle of the Three* by Tabitha Caplinger** (Christian Fantasy) The trilogy begins when Zoe Andrews discovers she is part of an ancient bloodline, she also learns that not all shadows are harmless interceptions of light. But Zoe, the daughter of the three, isn't just another descendant–she's the key to humanity's salvation.